P9-EEJ-989

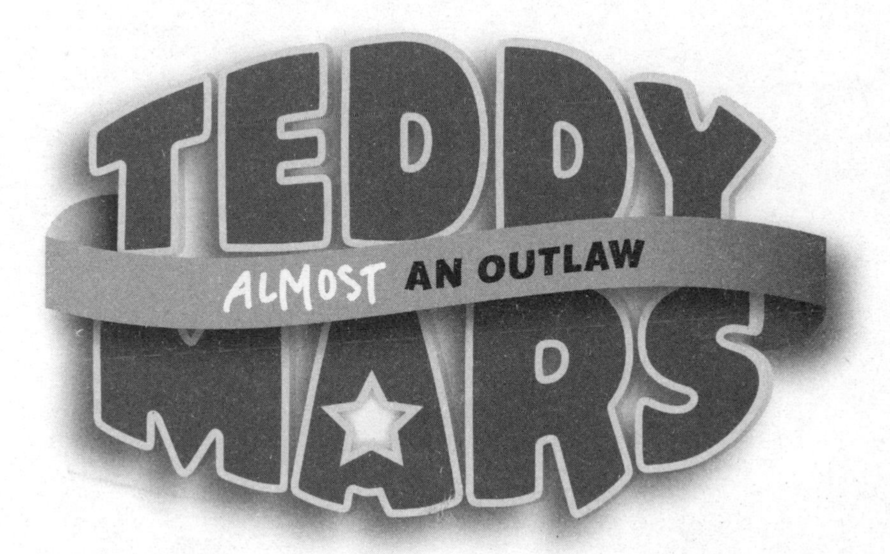
TEDDY
ALMOST AN OUTLAW
MARS

ALSO BY MOLLY B. BURNHAM

Teddy Mars Book #1:
Almost a World Record Breaker

Teddy Mars Book #2:
Almost a Winner

MOLLY B. BURNHAM

Illustrations by

TREVOR SPENCER

Katherine Tegen Books is an imprint of HarperCollins Publishers.

Teddy Mars Book #3: Almost an Outlaw

Library of Congress Control Number: 2016935933
ISBN 978-0-06-227816-6

Typography by Erin Fitzsimmons
17 18 19 20 21 CG/LSCH 10 9 8 7 6 5 4 3 2 1
❖
First Edition

To my husband, Sean Greene.
You are my Collaborator, Constructor,
Supreme Laugherator, and without a doubt,
one of my favorite Distractors of all time.

MOST WALNUTS

The day Lonnie, Viva, and I started breathing like Darth Vader was the same day we tried breaking the world record for cracking the most walnuts with only our heads.

Strange but true, it was not a coincidence.

Cracking walnuts with our heads was not the smartest record we've tried to break, and I'll be the first to say it was the most painful, but months ago we said we'd break a world record together—and we're not stopping until we do.

We've definitely had some distractions along the way, like collecting the most plastic bags with our classmates. I don't know if it was because of the plastic bags, or how many kids were involved, but that one almost ended our friendship. Luckily we sorted it out, and now we're back and stronger than ever.

THE EXTRAORDINARY FORCE OF OUR HEADS

This is why when Viva walks into my kitchen after school, plops down a bag of walnuts, and tells Lonnie and me her idea, we don't think twice. The fact that she kept it a secret from us in school all day makes it even better.

"But you've only brought twenty," Lonnie says. "The record must be higher."

I nod. "The record is 150." I know a lot of world records.

Viva rolls her eyes. "I know the record. This is just practice. First, we learn the technique; then we break the record."

"Good thinking." Lonnie smiles.

Our cat, Smarty Pants, meows loudly at me. I reach down to pet her, but she runs away.

Viva places a walnut in front of each one of us. "On the count of three," she says, "we bring the extraordinary force of our heads down onto those measly walnuts."

We do a high five, then count, "One. Two. Three!"

As it turns out, our heads are not so forceful, and the walnuts are not so measly. And once more, we prove that breaking a world record is way harder than it looks.

And that's when Lonnie closes his eyes and starts breathing like Darth Vader, which also proves that a head injury can make a person do weird things.

DARTH VADER BREATHING

Viva and I stare at Lonnie, who sounds like a combination of being underwater, being in an echo

chamber, and purring like Smarty Pants.

"Are you okay?" I ask as I wipe my eyes. Tears really make it hard to see. I reach in the freezer, grab three pieces of ice, and hand them around.

Lonnie takes the ice and keeps breathing in that raspy way.

"Are you going to tell us what is going on?" Viva squeaks, because pain makes it harder to talk.

"I'm breathing," Lonnie explains.

"Got that part," Viva says. "My question is, why are you breathing like Darth Vader?"

Lonnie stops breathing. "I read about this thing called deep breathing and how it helps with concentrating, calming down, and pain management, which is what I need right now."

"But why Darth Vader?" I ask.

Lonnie shrugs. "Darth Vader breathes more than anyone else in the world and he was powerful at using the Force. So he must have known something about deep breathing."

This is why Lonnie is my best friend, because he's just weird enough and just cool enough to think of something like Darth Vader breathing.

Before you know it all three of us are breathing like Darth Vader. The only distraction comes

from Smarty Pants's meows. We keep breathing and pretty soon, the pain is gone.

Viva looks at Lonnie. "You really are a Jedi."

He smiles, because if Lonnie could pick one thing to be, besides a world record breaker, he'd be a Jedi.

That's when The Destructor runs in, screaming his head off, and a whole different kind of pain crushes my head.

RULES FOR SURVIVING THE DESTRUCTOR

1. Hide all the things you love. (Or never see them in one piece again.)
2. Watch him like a hawk. (Or prepare to suffer the consequences.)
3. Trust him as far as you can throw him. (He's only five, and could probably be thrown pretty far, so I'm changing this one to: trust him as far as you can drop him.)

CAN BOY VERSUS THE DESTRUCTOR

About a month ago, The Destructor, or Jake, as the rest of my family calls him, taped twenty tin cans to his clothes and called himself Can Boy.

Since then he's taped them back on about a million times. Even duct tape gets destroyed by The Destructor.

My parents maintain that his can outfit is far better than what he's done in the past:

1. Living in a cat box.
2. Sticking feathers to himself with pigeon poo.

They might be right.

For now.

But I know The Destructor, and I know what he is capable of. No matter what he wants to be called, he'll always be The Destructor to me.

THE DESTRUCTION CONTINUES

So there we are, Lonnie, Viva, and me, all thinking about the power of breathing like Darth Vader, when The Destructor runs straight into me. I fall over and he and his tin cans fall on top of me. Grace follows right behind, holding up her camera and shouting, "Just one picture! I only need one!" My sister Grace is a photographer for her school newspaper. She takes her job very seriously.

"Come on, Jake!" Grace yells. "Stand still!"

The Destructor does not stand still; instead he leaps up, jumping from foot to foot.

"No!" The Destructor hollers back.

"Come on, Jake. You'll be famous."

"I don't want to be famous!"

Grace tries to grab him but The Destructor slips out of her grasp and dives into Smarty Pants's cat box. Months ago, when he basically lived in the cat box, my parents bought one just for him. But, of course, he doesn't go for that one.

He goes for the dirty one. The good news is he doesn't get far because halfway in his tin can outfit stops him.

The bad news is that Smarty Pants is inside doing what she does in there. The worse news is that Grace pulls him out by his feet, but before she can even focus her camera, The Destructor takes off, spraying cat litter all over the place.

By all over the place, I do mean all over me.

HARD TO BREATHE

I'm shaking cat litter out of my hair when Grace says, "Why didn't you stop him?" Then she asks, "What are you all up to?"

"Nothing," I say, hiding the walnuts we didn't crush under Mom's newspaper. It's always safer if Grace knows as little as possible.

"Then why are your foreheads all red?" She peers closer. "And swollen."

Grace holds up her camera and snaps away. It's clear from how we all cringe that being photographed is about as pleasant as breaking the record for kissing the most cobras (11). In other words, not at all.

Grace stops and looks at the pictures so far.

"Oh, never mind. I can't get a clear image of it. Next time I see you three, you better be doing something newsworthy!"

On her way out, Grace stomps on my foot. After photography, Grace's favorite thing to do is stomp on my feet.

While I'm doubled over in agony, Mom walks in. Smarty Pants meows again.

"Teddy? Can you feed Smarty Pants?" Mom asks as she walks out of the room, not noticing my suffering.

Lonnie says, "Don't forget to breathe."

"Like Darth Vader," Viva adds.

I do what they say because it worked so well the first time. But between the cat litter showering down on me from my hair, the foot that is probably broken, and Mom asking me to feed the cat, it's actually impossible to breathe at all.

THE ONLY PLACE TO THINK

In my house there's only one place to get any thinking done, and in fact, it's not in my house. It's in the pigeons' house next door.

That is where Lonnie, Viva, and I go to continue our world-record-breaking plans.

Grumpy Pigeon Man owns the pigeons. Mom likes me to call him Mr. Marney, but he likes Grumpy Pigeon Man, so we have a deal. I call him Grumpy Pigeon Man, feed his pigeons twice a day, and he pays me and calls me Tent Boy, because of how I lived in a tent for a while.

Grumpy Pigeon Man owns fifty-seven pigeons. That's quite a lot. They all live in a shed thing in his backyard. He calls it an aviary. It does have a screened-in porch section, where they spend most of their time. He calls it a loft. They are allowed to fly outside, but only when he's around.

There are lots of rules about the pigeons and how to take care of them, and Grumpy Pigeon Man likes to explain them over and over again. I let him because there's no point in stopping him. He wouldn't listen anyway.

RULES FOR GETTING ALONG WITH GRUMPY PIGEON MAN

1. Do what he says when he says it.
2. Don't talk too much.
3. Treat his pigeons like they are worth more to us than the largest diamond in the

universe, which happens to be a dwarf star fifty light-years away. It is estimated that that diamond is 2,500 miles across and is worth $16 undecillion, which looks like this in numbers: $16,000,000,000,000,000,000,000,000,000,000,000,000.

Treating his pigeons like this is not hard, because they are priceless to both Grumpy Pigeon Man and to me.

WHY HAVE RULES IF WE NEVER FOLLOW THEM?

Lonnie and Viva pull up two buckets, tip them over, and sit down. We're in the screened-in part—the loft. Unlike the inside section, which is full of cubbies—nesting boxes—and is enclosed, the loft has lots of perches for the pigeons to sit on. They talk to each other, preen their feathers, fly closer to one another, basically hang out like friends do.

Immediately, Obi-Wan Kenobi flies over and lands on Lonnie. Lando Calrissian flaps down onto Viva's knee. We named a lot of the pigeons after Star Wars characters.

Princess Leia flies over to me, flutters by my shoulder for a second, then settles right on top of my head. I don't move because I know better than to move when a pigeon is on my head. You don't want to startle a pigeon, unless you want to be pooed on.

Viva pets Lando. "I'm sorry about the walnuts."

Lonnie says, "It's our own fault. We forgot our rules." Lonnie shakes his head.

Of course, the rules.

Really we're about as good at following rules as we are about breaking records, which is lousy.

RULES FOR BREAKING A WORLD RECORD

1. It can't hurt.
2. It can't make us sick.
3. It can't cost a lot of money.

SILENT AND STINKY

Lando Calrissian flies off Viva's leg, replaced immediately by Admiral Ackbar.

Meanwhile Princess Leia is now pretty much nesting on my head.

"Maybe if we think about records we've tried, it will help us know what we should do."

Lonnie nods. "Good point." He holds up one finger. "We crushed eggs with our toes."

"Couldn't stand on our feet," Viva says.

Lonnie holds up two fingers. "Longest time doing jumping jacks."

"Couldn't move at all." Viva smiles. "I think I'm seeing a pattern."

"Most books balanced on our heads," Lonnie says.

"Too many bruises." Viva nods as she remembers that idea of hers.

"Most marshmallows eaten." Lonnie puts up four fingers.

"Toothaches, stomachaches, and you threw up." I point at Viva, but stay very still so I don't scare Princess Leia.

"What am I forgetting?" Lonnie asks.

"Oh!" Viva says. "There was the garlic."

"The garlic," Lonnie repeats. "That was the worst."

"We farted for hours!" Viva exclaims.

"And we were at school," I say.

"And they were silent," Viva adds.

"And stinky," Lonnie says.

Princess Leia, who is still settled on top of my head, coos loudly as if she remembers the stink, too.

And that's when a scream explodes from my house, loud enough to startle not just me, but Lonnie and Viva, and the pigeons. Princess Leia takes off, and as she flies away, she does the thing all pigeons do when they are scared: she poos.

And of course, it splats on me, which is gross, but is still not as bad as those farts.

THE SCREAMER

I have two goals in mind when I head back to my house. One is to wash the pigeon poo off my face, the other is to find out who screamed. Lonnie and Viva follow close behind. Somehow they escaped getting pooed on.

Lonnie smiles and says, "Considering how much good luck you have, you'd think we'd have broken a record together by now."

Lonnie has this whole theory about how being pooed on is good luck. I like the idea because I have the bad luck of being pooed on a lot, and it would be nice to think that it's all adding up to something great.

When we walk into the kitchen, I'm both surprised and not surprised.

I'm not surprised that The Destructor is in the kitchen making a mess.

I am surprised that The Destructor is in the middle of the floor making a mess with a pile of trash. I repeat: TRASH! Trash from the garbage can, which is tipped over and lying right beside him.

I'm not surprised because I knew he would take this Can Boy thing further.

I am surprised because Dad is standing in the doorway absolutely frozen with his mouth wide open, which has to mean that he was the screamer.

Right then, everyone else in the family clatters down the stairs, bumping into Dad like the record for most dominoes toppled by an individual (321,197).

"Oh, Jake," Dad says.

"How many times do I have to tell you, call me Can Boy!" The Destructor shakes his head at Dad. "And I'm recycling." He reaches into the garbage can next to him and pulls out a plastic lid. "This can be recycled."

That's when I notice that the trash around him is sorted into piles. One of the piles is trash, one is recycling, and one is old food scraps.

For the record, I'm a big fan of recycling. After all, it's the small things we do in this world that have a big effect.

Take for instance the tallest toothpick sculpture in *The Guinness Book of World Records*. Each toothpick is tiny, but all the toothpicks together, about 25,000 of them, make a 16-foot-8-inch-tall model of the Burj Khalifa tower, which happens to hold the record for the tallest building in the world. This means the person who made the toothpick sculpture broke a record with a record. Very cool.

But back to my point. I'm glad The Destructor

cares about the small stuff, I just wish he didn't take it so far.

SISTERS

Sharon holds her nose. "I am so glad I'm going to college next year." She walks back up the stairs, singing, "All by myself! I wanna beeee allll by myyyyyself!"

As Caitlin and Casey snap on their bike helmets, they say, "When you're older you can work for us." Besides talking at the same time, they collect trash on their bikes.

Maggie shrugs. "Running is definitely a better way to spend your free time." And leaves for a run.

Grace pulls out her camera. "My editor is going to love this." She clicks away. "I'm emailing these to her right away." And she dashes out.

My sisters clearly know that it's best to get away. I am about to do the same when Mom walks in with the phone up to her ear.

She freezes, and then says, "Can you hold on for one minute?" She closes her eyes and sighs.

Mom hands me a wet paper towel to wipe the poo off my face, which is very nice of her.

Mom brings the phone back to her ear. "Sorry about that," she says. She listens for a minute, then says, "Oh, they have excellent manners."

I wonder who she could be talking to, but more than that, I wonder who she could be talking about. It can't be my family, because good manners and us are as far apart as the two ends of the longest sausage in the world (38.99 miles).

Mom covers the phone and leans over to Dad, who is still frozen to the same spot. "Can you please take care of this?" she whispers, and walks out of the room.

Dad finally moves, picking up the garbage can so it's upright. "Jake," he says.

"Can Boy," The Destructor says, standing up.

Just then Mom calls Dad into the living room. "Teddy," Mom calls, "watch your brother for a minute."

"Watch The Destructor?" I repeat.

The Destructor gives me a smile, then stands up and reaches into the bowels of the garbage can, digging deeper and deeper until he tips all the way in.

"Help!" he shouts. "Help!" His feet flail around in the air.

"Do something," Lonnie says.

"Save him," Viva says.

"Do I have to?" I ask. They both push me forward.

"Okay," I say. Viva and Lonnie take the trash-can side. I take The Destructor's feet, and on the count of three we tip him upright and pull the can off. Trash pours out around our feet.

The Destructor stands there, dripping in garbage. "Thanks," he says. "I can always count on you."

Then he hugs me, and again, my thoughts drift to the longest sausage, and how much I wish there were 38.99 miles between The Destructor and me.

THAT QUESTION

"Mrs. Mars?" Lonnie calls. "I think Teddy needs you."

Mom walks back into the kitchen. She's not on the phone but I hear Dad talking in the other room. "What happened?" she asks as she picks off the stray bits of garbage on my clothes.

"Maybe if The Destructor's latest hobby wasn't rummaging through trash you wouldn't have to ask that question."

"You all have hobbies. I don't judge; I support."

It's true, she doesn't judge, and it's one of the best things about her.

HOBBIES MOM HAS SUPPORTED, BUT PROBABLY SHOULDN'T HAVE

1. Sharon (eighteen): Singing. (Especially in the bathroom.)
2. and 3. Caitlin and Casey (fifteen): Collecting trash on their bikes. (Because being twins isn't enough of a hobby.)
4. Maggie (fourteen): Running. (She should have been born a hamster.)
5. Grace (thirteen): Causing pain. (Especially to my feet.)
6. Me (ten): Breaking world records. (Since

I've only actually broken one, I guess I should say my hobby is *trying* to break world records.)

7. The Destructor (five): Doing anything that ruins my life. (And now digging through the trash.)

As I make this list, I can't help wondering how my parents put up with any of us.

DINNER AND THE DESTRUCTOR

Lonnie and Viva leave before I get cleaned up, which I totally understand. The smell of trash is pretty overwhelming. They'll be back tomorrow. As I've said before, we've got a world record to break.

Later that same night, after The Destructor takes his bath and my sisters get home from chorus, work, track, and whatever it is Grace does with her pictures, we all sit down for dinner.

Mom and Dad have a rule about family dinners. We have them. Now that I think about it, it might be their only rule, which is why my whole family is crowded around the dining room table. Everyone except The Destructor, who is eating under the table, in his cat box, with his tin can outfit on. Technically, only his bottom half is in the cat box, because his tin cans block him from getting all the way in.

There are a lot of reasons why this might be strange, but in our family it's strange because for a while The Destructor stopped eating in his cat box. We all thought he was done with it for good, but tonight for some strange reason he crawled back in.

When Sharon starts to complain about it, Mom makes the "cut off your head" signal, which means "don't talk about it, because he'll grow out of it if we don't make it feel special."

MARSHMALLOW NOSE BLOW

Strange but true, there is a world record for catching marshmallows in your mouth that have been shot out of someone else's nose. Really. It's called a marshmallow nose blow, and the record was shot from 17 feet 11 inches away. That's remarkably far, and totally gross.

The only thing grosser is the spinach-and-egg thing that Dad cooked. Not even a marshmallow up the nose is as gross as that.

GOOD NEWS VERSUS BAD NEWS

Mom and Dad keep giving each other funny looks. Their eyeballs are rolling around in their heads so much you'd think they were trying to break some record. It's obvious they have something to say, but they're not saying it. It's hard not to get nervous when your parents do stuff like this. The last time they acted this weird was when they told us they were having another baby, and now we have The Destructor.

Finally, I can't stand it anymore, so I blurt out, "Okay, what's going on?"

"Who said anything was going on?" Mom asks.

I give her my "who are you kidding" look.

Mom looks at Dad, he nods, and then she takes a deep breath. Not a Darth Vader breath, just a regular deep breath, like she's getting ready to tell us something important. "You're right, Teddy. We have some news."

The Destructor peers out from under the table and says, "No news is good news." Then shovels spinach and egg into his mouth.

"This is good news," Dad says.

Grace picks up her camera. "No one minds if I take some pictures while the news is being broken? If it is bad news, your expressions will be way better."

Caitlin and Casey look surprised. "So you're hoping for bad news?"

"I didn't say that," Grace explains. "I just said bad news makes better news."

Sharon says, "Sad songs are more popular."

Maggie nods. "Everyone likes stories where athletes mess up."

Mom clears her throat to get our attention. She smiles a big smile so we all know she really thinks this is good news.

"I got a job."

The Destructor shakes his head. "I knew it was bad news."

DEFINITELY BAD NEWS

For once I'm in total agreement with The Destructor, but I can't speak because I feel like I'm one of the three watermelons Olga Liashchuk crushed with her thighs in 14.65 seconds. Proving that people will do almost anything to break a record.

Dad says, "It's not that bad."

The Destructor pops up and takes more spinach and egg. "Yes, yes, it is." And he disappears under the table.

Again, I agree with him. But I also wonder how she could have done this and not talked to any of us. Not prepared us.

Mom frowns. "Well, I'm very excited. I haven't worked since Caitlin and Casey were born. A little enthusiasm would be welcome."

Sharon practically sings to Mom, "I think it's great!"

"Us too!" Caitlin and Casey agree.

Maggie gives a thumbs-up.

Grace walks around the table, putting her

camera in our faces and saying, "Don't hold back. Let the camera soak up your emotions."

This might be the only time that I wish that camera really *could* soak up emotions, because my eyes are feeling very damp.

COULD THIS GET ANY WORSE?

Dad taps on the table like a drum roll. "And the job is . . ."

Mom laughs. She plays along with Dad and starts drumming, too, then says in an announcer voice, "Animal control officer!"

It's clear from all our blank stares that none of us know why she's so excited about this job.

The Destructor sticks his head out from under the table. "You're going to control animals?" he asks. "Like at a circus?"

"No." Mom shakes her head. "I'll keep track of pets, make sure they're vaccinated, or help find them if they get lost. I'll also handle any complaints about animals."

"Who would complain about an animal?" The Destructor wonders, but no one answers him because Mom's explaining about the animals she means, like bears getting into the trash and skunks and raccoons. I'm only half listening because I'm thinking so hard about what we're going to do with Mom working. How will we survive? Who will take care of The Destructor? For that matter, who will take care of me?

Dad smiles. "This is going to be a big change for the family, which is why your mom and I think we'll need help."

My sisters' faces get all tight. They feel they don't need any help. This is usually true, but not always true.

"Just through the summer," Mom adds.

I swallow. The words finally come out of me. "Is Gran going to come live with us?" Gran is the only person who would make up for losing Mom.

"No," Mom says. "Sadly she can't, but we have another relative who can."

Dad does another drum roll on the table, but this time it makes me worried. "Aunt Ursula is coming to live with us!"

"You mean Great-Aunt Ursula?" I ask. "Dad's aunt Ursula? The one who came before?"

Mom and Dad nod.

And just like the record for loudest roar in a stadium (142.2 decibels), every one of my sisters and I scream at the same time.

COULD THIS GET ANY WORSE? PART 2

Mom says, "She's not that bad."

My sisters and I all start talking at once. We know exactly how bad she is.

"Who's Aunt Ursula?" The Destructor asks. I'm reminded that he was only a baby the last time she was here. He climbs out from under the table, puts his hand on his belly and says, "I don't feel so good." A second later, he opens his mouth and throws up all over me.

It turns out the only thing grosser than spinach and egg is spinach-and-egg throw-up.

Grace holds up her camera and says, "It doesn't get better than this."

Obviously, I totally disagree.

COULD THIS GET ANY WORSE? PART 3

Later that same night, after I'm finally cleaned up, I walk into my bedroom, where The Destructor is snuggled up in his bed with Mom.

She's saying, "It's going to be wonderful. I'll go to work and Aunt Ursula will be here to take care of you, and to help Teddy get to school."

The Destructor says, "And she's staying until the end of summer?"

Mom nods.

"Until I start school?"

"Start school?" I ask.

Mom nods again. "Jake starts kindergarten in September. You'll be in the same school." Mom says it like this is the best thing ever. I pull the covers over my head, because next to Mom getting a job, Aunt Ursula moving in, and being upchucked on, The Destructor going to my school is still the worst.

"What if I don't go to school? Will you quit your job?"

Mom smiles. "How about we get through one thing at a time?"

Mom kisses The Destructor good night, then comes to me.

"Are you sure he's okay?" I ask.

"He's fine." She leans down and whispers, "You know, I'm going to need your help, too."

"I don't like where this is going," I say.

"I'll need you to take care of your brother."

"I thought I said I didn't like where this was going."

"I love you," she says, which isn't possible since she's ruining my life. She kisses me and walks out of the room.

As soon as she closes the door, The Destructor hops out of his bed and climbs into mine. "Okay, why is this lady such bad news?"

I shake my head. "Where do I begin?"

GREAT-AUNT URSULA

The Destructor begs me some more to tell him about Aunt Ursula. "I won't fall asleep until I know something."

To be honest, I don't feel like talking about Aunt Ursula at all, so I do some Darth Vader breathing to calm down. When I open my eyes, The Destructor is staring at me with begging eyes, so I say, "Technically she is our great-aunt Ursula, but we just call her aunt."

"What's she like?"

"Do you know Mary Poppins?"

He nods and smiles.

"She's nothing like that."

His smile falls off his face.

"You know Queen Latifah?" I ask.

"I love her," he says. "She's so funny!"

"Aunt Ursula is nothing like her, either." I stop talking for a second. I haven't thought about Aunt Ursula for years. The last time she came, I was five and was terrified of her. She wanted everything done in a certain way, and she wasn't afraid to tell us how it was supposed to be done.

Instead I say, "Her teeth are made from shards of glass and you only see them when she's nibbling on the bones of children. Or telling you her rules."

"That's not true," The Destructor says, but his eyes are big, and I'm on a roll now so I keep talking. "She has arms that stretch farther than a real person's so she can grab you if you break one of her rules."

"I hate rules," he whispers.

"She has ears like an owl that can hear you wherever you are in the house—especially if you're breaking one of her rules." I have to admit, after all the suffering The Destructor has caused, it's fun to scare him. "She has a nose like a wolf and can smell whatever you are doing. Especially if you are breaking one of her rules."

The Destructor's eyes are even bigger, and he asks, "How many rules does she have?"

"Aunt Ursula has more rules than *The Guinness Book of World Records* has records."

"What's one of her rules?" he asks. I can tell he doesn't really want to know, but he has to ask.

I think for a minute. "If you are asked to do something, do it. Or else she will use mind control to make you do it anyway."

The Destructor leaps out of bed, screaming, "MOOOOOOOOOM!"

I smile to myself, feeling like my job is done, and also like I finally understand Darth Vader.

SCARED AS THE DESTRUCTOR

I hear The Destructor whining that he wants to sleep with Mom tonight.

Mom says, "She doesn't eat children. She's related to Dad." But he doesn't stop begging, so she agrees. Mom is a real pushover for The Destructor.

But as I lie in the dark all I can think about is Aunt Ursula and the stuff I said about her—not the made-up stuff like the teeth, the arms, the ears, or the nose—but the stuff about her rules. I was only five when she was last here, but her rules were endless and they made no sense.

That was five years ago! She must have a thousand more rules now.

"Oh, great," I whisper to my pillow. "Now I'm scared." I climb out of bed and walk down the hall.

Mom looks at me and says, "You too?" She moves over to make room. "Dad will have to sleep in the guest room."

I can't believe this, but I actually feel bad about The Destructor, so I say, "I'm sorry I scared you."

The Destructor looks surprised. "I'm not scared; I'm sad." And he reaches over and hugs Mom.

Dad sleeps in the guest room, but I end up on the floor because it turns out The Destructor is a real squirmer.

By squirmer, I actually mean kicker.

I still wake up on time to feed the pigeons. It's like I have an alarm clock inside my head that instead of going cuckoo, goes coo, coo, just like pigeons.

GRUMPY PIGEON MAN'S RULES ABOUT PIGEONS

1. Pigeons like quiet. (I try to be quiet.)
2. Keep the door closed. (I try to close it quietly.)
3. Feed the pigeons for ten minutes and ten minutes only. (I'm very good at doing this.)
4. Give the pigeons fresh water twice a day. (Pigeons like to drink and take baths.)
5. Do not name the pigeons after any more

Star Wars characters. (I've never promised I would do this.)

PIGEONS VERSUS SADNESS

Usually, I love being with the pigeons, but today I shuffle over. I pour their food and water. I count to six hundred seconds, which is what ten minutes equals in seconds and is how long they get to eat, and then I take the food away.

Obi-Wan Kenobi flies down to say hello. He coos at me and walks up and down my leg. I have to say, one of the great things about pigeons is they have no idea if you're happy or sad and they don't care. But the even greater thing about pigeons is that when you are sad, just being with them makes you feel better.

THE COUNTDOWN BEGINS

When I walk into the kitchen, The Destructor is all by himself eating cereal in his cat box. Again, half in his cat box and half out. I think about suggesting he take off the tin cans, but he looks so sad that I can't.

"You okay, Destructor?" I ask.

"Can Boy!" he says, scooping the cereal into his mouth. "And no! I'm not okay. What are we going to do when Mom goes to work?" His voice gets all shaky and milk dribbles down his chin and then he starts to cry.

And I admit, I don't know what to say. Usually, he cries over things I don't care about, but this time I feel the same. Luckily, Sharon walks in. I figure she's going to college soon, so she'll know what to do. Then I notice she's not singing. Even I know things are bad if Sharon isn't singing. She collapses into a chair.

When I hear Caitlin and Casey coming downstairs I perk up. They're always cheerful. But one look at them tells me they feel as bad as we do. And that goes for all my sisters. Maggie walks into the kitchen instead of running. She's not even wearing her sneakers. When Grace shows up, she doesn't hold up her camera or even try to stomp on my foot.

This is the worst morning ever. And the countdown has only just begun.

(Of course, I don't actually know when Mom starts work, so it's not much of a countdown.)

MOM'S RULE

Mom has a rule about breakfast. The rule is: make your own.

But this morning when Mom walks into the kitchen, she looks around, then wraps an apron around her waist, and grabs a pad of paper and a pencil. She pretends to be chewing gum, and says, "What can I get ya?"

Strange but true, Sirius holds the record for the brightest star. It is 24 times brighter than the sun. Suddenly, my whole family shines as bright as that star, even The Destructor, who points to his stomach and says, "I think I've got room right here for more food."

We give Mom our orders and she says stuff like, "You want coffee with that? No extra charge," which cracks us all up because none of us drink coffee, not even Sharon, and we aren't going to pay her. She sets glasses on the table. "Juice comes with that. No extra charge."

Thinking about juice makes

me a little sad because it gets me thinking about Aunt Ursula and her prune juice rule, which is to drink it every day. Blech!

But I forget all about that as Mom hustles around the kitchen cooking up scrambled eggs, and poached eggs, and fried eggs, because none of my sisters like eggs the same way.

"For the kid who hates eggs." Mom plops down a bowl of oatmeal for me.

"And Cheerios for the kid wearing the cans."

"Can Boy," he says. "The name is Can Boy."

"Sure, kid." She winks. "Whatever you say."

"Thanks." I hug Mom as Dad walks in.

"Is there anything for me?" he asks.

Mom points to the pile of dishes and says, "A sink full of dishes."

Then she starts making our lunches.

And all I can think is, how will we survive without her?

SHE MEANS BUSINESS

The world record for busiest train station is Shinjuku station in Tokyo, Japan. The station has two hundred exits and serves about 3.64 million passengers every day. That place has got to be crowded and difficult to get through. Strange but true, first thing in the morning, our classroom feels a lot like that train station. When we walk in, we all rush in to hang up our backpacks, put away lunches, and pull out homework. And even though our class doesn't have 3.64 million kids, I still get a foot in my shin, and when I lean down to rub it, I get a lunchbox whacked in my face.

Lonnie stuffs his lunch into the cubby next to mine and sees the pain wash over me. "Don't forget to breathe." He smiles.

Viva squirms her way to safety as Lonnie and I follow. Usually, I get straight to talking about possible records to break, but today all I want to do is tell them about Mom, her new job, and Aunt Ursula.

"You won't believe what happened yesterday."

"The Destructor got stuck in the trash can again?" Lonnie asks.

"You've decided to break a record for most showers in a row?" Viva laughs, cracking up at her own joke. Actually, that's not a bad idea, and she doesn't even know about the one last night.

Before I can get any further Ms. Raffeli claps

her hands. Everyone races for the rug and plunges into a circle. Lewis, in his excitement to get to his spot, elbows me in the ribs. I double over.

Lonnie looks at me and says, "Darth Vader breathing."

Viva nods. "It's the only answer."

Which is true, and I do it, but I can't tell them my news if I'm breathing like this.

"Okay, quiet down," Ms. Raffeli announces. "You too, Teddy." By the way her eyebrows rise up her forehead I know she means business.

Lonnie whispers, "Can it wait until lunch?"

Strange but true, the record for greatest weight lifted by the hair is 179 pounds 10.82 ounces and was broken by an eighty-three-year-old. If an eighty-three-year-old man can lift that much weight with his hair, then I can wait until lunch to tell Lonnie and Viva my news.

It will be painful, but I'll get through.

EYEBROWS WIN EVERY TIME

"So little time and so much to do," Ms. Raffeli says, grabbing a tissue. "Allergies," she explains. "They are especially bad this time of year." She

blows her nose vigorously, then says, "There is only one week until the end of school."

"Is that including today?" Ny asks, looking at the calendar.

"I don't think so," Serena says, tossing her hair over her shoulder and whacking me in the face.

Lonnie says, "The last day of school is the Monday after this one."

"That's what I was going to say," Lewis says.

"So that means it's more than a week," Angus says, pulling his shirt over his knees and hopping around in circles.

"Only if you're counting today," Cornelio explains.

"And the last day is a half day," Jasmine B. chimes in.

"I never know how to count half days," Jasmine H. adds.

I shake my head. "I thought I knew how many days were left."

Lonnie leans over. "We've got six and a half days, including today, until—"

That's when we all notice Ms. Raffeli's eyebrows crawling up her face like that fastest caterpillar in the world (15 inches per second), which is superfast. And even though we're all still wondering how many days are left, the caterpillar eyebrows win and we stop talking.

THAT WOULD BE CRAZY

Ms. Raffeli wipes her eyes, and then pulls out a piece of paper. "A message from our principal," she says. "To the fourth grade class entering fifth grade." She clears her throat. "Next year you will each be given a kindergarten buddy. You will act as a friend, a teacher, even perhaps like an older sibling. This incoming student can count on you through the whole year to guide them, read to them, be there for them, and most important, to help them transition to our wonderful community."

Everyone around me nods in excitement like the pigeons do when I come to feed them. Obviously the rest of the class likes this idea. But they don't have a little brother like mine. Next year, The Destructor will be here. My heart sinks. It's bad enough sharing a room with him, now I'll have to share a school with him. But then I think of something worse: What if they pair him with me? I didn't know it was possible to feel this bad.

Ms. Raffeli smiles. "Today we will start by writing a welcome letter to your buddy."

I take a few Darth Vader breaths to calm down, and tell myself that no teacher would put The Destructor and me together. That would be crazy.

But then Ms. Raffeli holds up a list with two columns of names. And clearly, right there is my name, and across from it, Jake Mars—The Destructor is my buddy!

PENCILS

Ms. Raffeli explains to me that a lot of thought went into this decision, and that even my parents were brought in on it. "My parents knew?!" I'm so mad I actually feel like Darth Vader and I'm not even breathing like him.

Ms. Raffeli says, "Your parents were supposed

to talk to you about it. We all felt that Jake needs extra help during this transition, the kind of help that only his brother can give."

I don't have anything to say, and even if I did, I'm so mad I can't speak, so I walk away.

I can't believe my parents knew this and didn't talk to me. Just like they knew Mom was applying for jobs but didn't talk about it, and they knew that if she got the job Aunt Ursula would come, but didn't talk to us about it.

Even though I'm super mad, I spend the morning writing a welcome letter to The Destructor. This is not easy, especially because my pencil breaks about a million times. I guess I'm pressing down a little harder than usual. Ms. Raffeli ends up leaving a box of pencils on my desk. I guess she understands.

THE NOTE

Finally, it's time for lunch. Lonnie, Viva, and I head straight for our table in the corner next to the trash can.

It is June and the warm weather makes the trash smell a little worse than usual. This is fine

with me because I like a quiet lunch.

Lonnie and Viva don't say anything as we unpack our lunches. Viva takes out a sandwich, celery, a peach, and a cookie. Lonnie takes out a sandwich, carrots, an apple, and a cookie.

I'm expecting my normal crummy lunch, but today it's different. There's red pepper and hummus and cheese and crackers, and my sandwich is not like any sandwich I've ever seen before. I hold it up for Lonnie and Viva.

"Stop right there," Viva says.

Lonnie shakes his head. "Your sandwich is shaped like a star!"

Viva touches the bread. "It's not moldy or stale."

Lonnie notices something sticking out of my lunch bag. He pulls out a piece of paper, and his eyes get bigger. "Your mom wrote you a note?"

I unfold it carefully because nothing like this has ever happened to me before.

Have a record breaker of a day!

Lonnie looks worried. "Teddy? Is everything okay?"

Viva frowns. “Are you moving?”

I take a deep breath and blink a bunch of times. I wonder if I have allergies, too. “My mom got a job.”

THE FORCE

Lonnie and Viva freeze. They don’t blink. They don’t chew, which is not easy since they both have food in their mouths. It feels so nice to tell my best friends. They know how life-changing this is.

“And?” Viva asks, then starts chewing. “What’s the big deal?”

Strange but true, there’s a world record for

a dog named Purin who caught 14 small soccer balls using only her paws. That dog had a lot to learn before she could break that record. You'd think if a dog could learn how to catch balls with her paws, that Viva could learn about me.

I ignore her question and explain about Mom's job at the animal control agency. They think it's cool because she'll be working with animals, which it is. Then I tell them about her making breakfast.

Lonnie says, "Breakfast, a nice lunch, and a note? She feels really bad."

"She should," I say.

"Why?" Viva asks. "I don't get it. My mom has always worked and we get along just fine. And Lonnie, your mom works and you don't have any problems."

Lonnie stares at Viva like she's crazy. "But it's the Mars family. They're not normal." Lonnie understands my family so well, and I really appreciate that about him. "What are they going to do with The Destructor?"

"Oh!" Viva's face lights up with understanding. "I didn't think about him."

"But wait, there's more," I say. "My aunt Ursula is moving in."

Lonnie shivers. "Aunt Ursula?"

"Who's Aunt Ursula?" Viva asks. "And how bad can she be?"

I explain who she is just as Lonnie pushes his food away. "I didn't go to Teddy's house the whole time she was there. Too hard to remember all her rules."

Even Viva knows that means something, because not only does Lonnie get along with everyone, he's also really good at rules.

"How am I going to survive?" I ask.

Lonnie puts his hand on my shoulder. "You lived 162 days in a tent. You have the Force."

Viva smiles and gives me a thumbs-up. "You just need to remember how to use it."

BEFORE WE LEAVE

At the end of the day, Ms. Raffeli races around, picking up pencils and glue sticks, finding lost lunch boxes, and admiring the work we did. Then she freezes. "Oops! I almost forgot."

She claps her hands. "This summer there will be an exciting project. You will have the opportunity to paint a mural on a wall outside our very own city hall. Our art teacher, Ms. Cecile, will lead the mural project. As an added bonus, our kindergarten buddies are invited to join in on the fun. Permission forms go home today. I need them back before the end of school!"

Viva leans over. "That sounds cool."

"I'd totally do that," Lonnie says.

"Stay focused, people!" I snap. "This summer is all about breaking another record, and no one is going to stop us."

They nod.

And then I remember that Mom is going back to work, and that Aunt Ursula will be staying with us. What will that be like? I start doing the Darth Vader breathing again. Ms. Raffeli looks up. "Teddy, are you all right?"

"It's that breathing thing I told you about."

"Does it have to be so noisy?"

"I think the noise helps, right, Lonnie?"

Lonnie nods.

Ms. Raffeli blinks a few times. "I can't believe it's almost the end of the year." She sniffs and starts passing out the permission slips. When she comes to me, she says, "Goodbye, Teddy," and hugs me.

"Ms. Raffeli, it's only the weekend. I'll be back on Monday."

She sighs. "I know, but—"

I reach over and give her hug. "I understand," I say, because I do. Change is hard, and Ms. Raffeli is about to go through a really big change. And so am I. We'll both need all the help we can get. "Don't forget the Darth Vader breathing."

"Thanks," she says. "And don't forget the form for the mural project. I think you'd love it."

I take it to be polite.

SMARTY PANTS

It's Saturday morning and the only thing Lonnie, Viva, and I have planned for the whole weekend is to break records. Mom puts The Destructor to work emptying all the trash cans in the house. This seems like a disaster waiting to happen, but she says, "Do you want to do it?" which is clearly a trick question, so I smile and offer Lonnie and Viva an apple.

When Lonnie and Viva congratulate Mom on her job, her eyes light up like she's one of the 1,070 sparklers used for the most sparklers lit at the same time world record. Technically, this is a group record. I am not a fan of group records, but this one is cool. Anyway, it's clear that Mom would like to hang out more and talk about her new job, but The Destructor's screams send her running upstairs.

Viva pulls out paper and pen. "We need to make a list of possible records to break."

Smarty Pants jumps up and lies right on top of the paper.

"Shoo, Smarty Pants," I say, pushing her off the table.

"She's so cute." Viva leans down and pets her.

Smarty Pants meows and walks away. And then comes back and does the same thing again.

Lonnie looks at her. "It's like she's trying to tell us something."

"What could she possibly want?" I ask.

But before we can figure out what Smarty Pants wants, Sharon and Jerome walk in. Jerome is her boyfriend and also Lonnie's big brother. We all agree he has gotten way nicer now that they are dating. I wish I could say the same for Sharon.

"We'll be in the bathroom," Sharon says.

Lonnie, Viva, and I all say, "Ewww!" at the same time.

"Practicing for the graduation song," Jerome adds.

Sharon explains, "Singing sounds best in the bathroom."

"It's the acoustics," Jerome says.

I don't know why they're telling us all this, and I'm pretty sure Smarty Pants feels the same because she meows at them until they leave the kitchen.

After they're gone, Viva taps the paper. "Any world record suggestions?"

That's when the singing starts. "Morning has broooooooken. Like the first morrrr-or-or-ning."

Smarty Pants joins in. I pet her. "Don't worry," I say. "She'll be going away to college soon." This does not help Smarty Pants, who stands in the middle of the room and howls just as Mom walks in.

"Teddy, did anyone think to feed Smarty Pants?" She grabs a can, opens it, and dumps the food into her bowl. Smarty Pants runs over and eats as if she hasn't eaten in days, which I know is not true because Mom fed her last night. I saw her do it. I hold my nose because cat food does not smell good.

"Why would we do it?" I ask. "That's your job."

Mom makes a sound that is a lot like a Darth Vader breath and I wonder why she needs to calm down. Her life is perfect. "I'll be mowing the grass," she says, and leaves.

Viva leans over and whispers, "Canned cat food is gross."

"Cat food is the worst," I whisper back. "That's a big reason not to feed the cat."

Lonnie leans in and whispers, "And parents like having jobs."

Lonnie has an excellent point.

RULES ABOUT PARENTS

1. Keep them busy. (A bored parent is a dangerous parent.)
2. Keep your room messy. (Parents need something to complain about.)
3. Give them jobs, like laundry, cleaning up, feeding the cat. (It makes them feel useful.)
4. Do what they want sometimes. (They like to feel loved.)

CAT RECORDS

The sound of Smarty Pants licking up her food fills the room. And that's when it hits me.

"Smarty Pants!" I say. "Why didn't we ever think of it before? We could break a record with Smarty Pants." I grab a copy of *The Guinness Book of World Records* and we circle up around it.

Lonnie finds the first cat record. "The most popular cat in politics."

Viva reads over his shoulder. "Socks was owned by President Clinton and received 75,000 pieces of mail every week from 1992 to 2000."

I shake my head. "We'll never break that one. Smarty Pants doesn't know that many people."

"Or have any interest in politics." Viva laughs and then reads another record. "Oldest cat: Creme Puff, 38 years 3 days."

"Smarty Pants is only twelve," I say.

Viva does the math. "So all we have to do is wait another twenty-six years."

Lonnie shakes his head. "I'd really like to break a record before I turn thirty-six."

We flip through the other records. There's the first domesticated cat (9,500 years ago), the most traveled cat (600,000 miles), the greatest mouser

(28,899 mice killed). Clearly, we can't break any of those.

Then Lonnie says, "How about longest fur on a cat? It's 10.11 inches."

Viva nods. "That's the one!"

MEASURING FUR

We spend fifteen minutes plying Smarty Pants with cat treats so she'll sit still long enough for us to measure her fur, only to discover that it's only two inches all over, which won't break any record, although we might have broken one for the most scratches inflicted on three kids by one cat!

CAT RECORDS PART 2

Sadly, by the time we recovered from our scratches, Viva's mom called and said she had to come home, that she wanted to have a little mother-daughter time with her.

So Lonnie and Viva come back today. They're later than I hoped, though, because Lonnie's grandparents were passing through and wanted to visit.

When they finally arrive, we go over cat record options. Basically, we don't have any.

"There's only one thing to do," Lonnie says.

Viva nods. "Make one up."

"How about longest time to run in circles?" Lonnie asks. "My grandmother showed me the funniest video today of a cat chasing its tail. It went on a really long time. If we could get Smarty Pants to do that, we'd have a record."

As the three of us jump up to look for a way to get Smarty Pants to chase her tail, Mom walks through. She's on the phone. She looks at me and walks out.

I don't have to wonder who Mom is talking to because it can only be one person. I don't ask Mom when Aunt Ursula is coming because I don't want to know. I also don't ask Mom when she starts work because I don't want to know that either.

All I want is to break a record with Lonnie and Viva. So I'm going to do just that and ignore the rest. And when Viva pulls out the shoelace from her sneakers and dangles it in front of Smarty Pants and Smarty Pants starts chasing it, I know exactly what will happen.

IT'S ALL GOING SO WELL

Lonnie watches the clock and counts the seconds. "Twenty-two. Twenty-three. Twenty-four."

Viva spins the shoelace and Smarty Pants runs in circles chasing it.

"You can do it, Smarty Pants," I say. And I really believe she can. She's awesome at chasing a string. I never knew she could do this for so long.

But then The Destructor runs in, his tin can clothes clanging against one another. "Guess what!" he yells. Smarty Pants takes one look at him and runs away. I would, too, but The Destructor hugs me so I can't move.

"Never mind," he squeals. "You'll never guess. I'm coming to your school tomorrow! Mom just told me. It's visiting day!" He lets go of me. "I can't wait. Mom says you're my buddy and I don't have anything to worry about. And I know it's true." He hugs me one more time, then grabs the shoelace from Viva and says, "I'll throw this away." Before Viva can tell him it's from her sneakers he dumps it in the trash and walks out of the room.

"Breathe," Viva says. "Just breathe."

"I don't think I can," I squeak.

Lonnie puts an arm around me. "We'll help out."

"Even with your awesome Jedi skills I don't think it will make a difference."

Lonnie thinks about this and then nods, because he knows I am right.

MORNINGS ARE HECTIC

Two parents, five sisters, two bathrooms, and me never goes well. Add The Destructor to the mix, and it's really bad.

The Destructor and I are standing in the hall waiting for Grace to get out of the bathroom. "You can't go to school like that," I say.

"Like what?"

"In tin cans."

"Why not?" The Destructor asks.

"Because there are rules at school. Things like walking quietly in the halls, raising your hand, and last but not least, wearing real clothes."

"These are real clothes."

"It's a rule," I say.

"Maybe I'll break the rules," he says.

"You can't break rules," I explain. "It's not legal."

"Maybe I won't go to school."

Mom walks up. "What do you mean, you won't go to school?"

"Teddy says I'm not allowed to wear my tin cans. It's a rule."

Mom gives me a look. "You know how much I love you, right, Jake?"

"Can Boy," he corrects.

She smiles. "You know how much I love you, but you will go to school. Even if I have to change the rule about tin cans."

His eyes get really big. "You can do that?"

"If I have to."

I don't know if Mom can change the rule, but out of anyone I know, she's probably the only one who could.

And if she did, I can honestly say it would definitely feel like she's trying to break a world record for most annoying parent!

SPECIAL TREATMENT

Because The Destructor is coming to school today, Mom drives us. In the car, she explains to The Destructor how I will take him to the kindergarten line, and how he will spend half the day in kindergarten, but will see me a lot.

The Destructor doesn't look worried at all, in fact, he smiles, but Mom adds, "And if you need anything, Teddy will be there, because he's your buddy."

I groan. Mom looks at me in the rearview

mirror. "Teddy, there are some rules to being a big brother. And one of them is to help out sometimes."

I can tell by her voice that she's serious, so I don't say anything, but I can't help wondering when he'll help me. Actually, I already know the answer. It will be the same day I break the record for largest collection of navel fluff, also known as belly-button lint.

In other words, never.

MS. RAFFELI VERSUS PRINCESS LEIA

As we walk up to the kindergarten line, he stops. "I don't want to go there."

"But that's what you do on visiting day," I say.

"I'm not going there."

"Destructor, you have to."

He shakes his head. "You're my buddy. I'm staying with you. All day."

I look for Mom, but she's already driven off. I grab The Destructor by his arm and start to pull him to the kindergarten line. He melts to the ground.

"Fine," I say. "Come on." He pops up and runs to my line, where Lonnie and Viva are waving.

They give The Destructor the high five when we arrive.

"Isn't he supposed to be with the kindergarteners?" Viva looks confused.

"Yup," I say.

"Not going?" Lonnie asks.

I shake my head. "Ms. Raffeli can sort it out."

But today Ms. Raffeli doesn't meet us outside, so we walk into school, through the hallway, up the stairs, and into my classroom. The Destructor is totally quiet the whole time. He doesn't scream, he doesn't touch the art on the walls. Of course there's still the clatter of his cans. He can't hide that.

In the classroom, The Destructor weaves into the chaos. He finds a hook and takes off the empty backpack he insisted on bringing. Lonnie, Viva, and I watch him like we're witnessing the highest blindfolded tightrope crossing (557.89 feet), which is very high and would be very stressful. But he makes it out unhurt and bounds over to the rug just as a foot collides with my shin. Lonnie and Viva sit next to him, but when I come he pushes Viva over so I have a place. A minute later Ms. Raffeli sits in her chair.

"Oh, Jake!" she says. "You startled me! It's kindergarten visiting day, isn't it?"

The Destructor smiles a huge smile. "Yup!" he says.

"Usually that means being in kindergarten."

He keeps smiling. "I'm staying here. And I like you." He reaches out and grabs Ms. Raffeli's hand. Her eyebrows shoot up her forehead and stop when they're as tall as the tallest sand castle (45 feet 10.25 inches).

Ms. Raffeli and I have a special relationship. Mostly because she knows my family very well since she has taught every single one of my sisters. This means I don't have to explain anything to her. She knows it all. She's also a real stickler for following school rules, so I am sure she will get The Destructor where he is supposed to be.

She looks at me. "Don't worry. I'll take care of it." She walks to the class phone to call the principal.

Lonnie says, "If there was a battle between Ms. Raffeli and Princess Leia, I know whose side I'd want to be on."

"Duh, Ms. Raffeli," Viva says.

We all agree because when it comes to Ms. Raffeli, there's no stopping her.

MS. RAFFELI VERSUS PRINCESS LEIA PART 2

While Ms. Raffeli is on the phone, The Destructor makes himself comfortable on the rug, and all my classmates circle around him and ask about his tin cans.

"First off, I like to be called Can Boy."

Lewis says, "I knew that."

I let out a Darth Vader breath.

"Do you like to recycle?" Ny asks.

"Totally," he says.

Jasmine B. points to his tin can shirt. "How long did it take you to make that?"

"Days," The Destructor says. "Maybe even months. Probably close to a year."

I shake my head, but decide not to correct him. No one would believe that he could do something like that in minutes.

And Jasmine H. asks, "Do those cans get uncomfortable?"

"Only when I lie down, and sometimes when I'm sitting up. Also when I laugh."

Serena flips her hair in my face. "Your brother is adorable."

Cornelio says, "He's one of a kind."

Angus hops over with his shirt pulled down over his knees. "Want to hop with me?"

And The Destructor pops up and starts hopping with Angus. He can't pull his tin can shirt over his knees but besides that he imitates Angus perfectly.

Ms. Raffeli walks back. "It's all settled."

I breathe a sigh of relief.

"He will stay with us this morning."

"But—" I start to say.

Ms. Raffeli stops me. "Don't worry. Because you're his buddy anyway, he was going to spend time with you. We'll just do it here instead of kindergarten."

She looks at The Destructor and Angus, who are still hopping. "I will need your help with him today, as both his buddy and his big brother." She pauses and we watch him hop around the room. "You'll probably need to control him a little bit."

Control him? Be his buddy? Act like a big brother? Who do people think I am?

There's only one person who could do all that, and that's Yoda. And the chances of me turning into an over-eight-hundred-year-old little green guy with big ears who can use the Force like nobody else in the universe is a lot to ask. Even for a record breaker like me.

Ms. Raffeli sits down. Angus hops back to the rug, and amazingly The Destructor follows him. He settles down in a spot next to me. Ms. Raffeli reaches behind her and pulls out a large plastic bag.

"Mystery bag!" we all cry out. Ms. Raffeli always starts a new unit the same way, with the mystery bag, and with us using clues from the bag to guess what the next unit will be. Considering we have so few days of school left, I can't imagine what more we need to learn. But Ms. Raffeli clearly has something to teach us.

The Destructor looks at me. "This is so great," he says. "I don't know why you ever complain about school."

Everyone laughs, even Ms. Raffeli. My face gets hot. The Destructor smiles. "I think they like me," he whispers in my face.

Ms. Raffeli holds out the bag. "Who wants to go first?" she asks. And right then and there I think maybe I do have a little Yoda in me, because I know without a doubt that something is going to happen. And it does. The Destructor rushes up, grabs the bag, and dumps all the clues out on the floor. We all watch, frozen to our spots as if we're living through the longest ice age, which

took place more than 2.3 billion years ago and lasted about 70 million years.

Finally Ms. Raffeli unfreezes and says, "I thought you were going to watch him for me."

I have to admit, it's really nice that Ms. Raffeli thinks I can keep him under control. At the start of the year I'm pretty sure she didn't think I could control myself.

It makes me feel proud of the progress I've made, but she and I both know it would take a whole ice age to get The Destructor under control.

MYSTERY BAG

After we recover from the destruction that The Destructor caused, Ms. Raffeli decides we'll do mystery bag a little differently, and lets us just dig through the pile of clues.

Cornelio pulls out a stuffed animal that's a bird.

"A measuring tape," Lonnie says as he grabs it off the rug.

Viva holds up a banana in a plastic bag.

Ny pulls out a copy of *The Guinness Book of World Records*! "Was this yours, Ms. Raffeli?"

Ms. Raffeli nods. "From when I was a kid."

It's not the right time, but I have to get a closer look at that book.

Jasmine B. and Jasmine H. hold up a picture of them on the monkey bars from the beginning of the year.

Crystal finds a figurine of the Empire State Building from the trip she took to New York City over spring vacation. And Angus pulls out a plain old plastic bag, like the ones our class used when we tried to break the record for largest collection of plastic bags.

Serena holds up a small plastic skunk. She smiles at me. "Remember when you got skunked, Teddy?"

I can feel my face get hot again.

Jasmine B. and Jasmine H. laugh. “That was funny.”

“And stinky,” Cornelio says.

“I wasn’t stinky,” I say. “I didn’t come back until the stink was gone.”

“That’s what you think,” Lonnie and Viva say at the exact same time, which makes everyone burst into laughter, including me.

“Ms. Raffeli.” Lewis raises his hand. “I know what this unit is.”

Lewis always says this, but Lewis knowing this is like me breaking the record for being the oldest gymnast in the world. It’s not going to happen.

“It’s things we’ve done this year,” Lewis shouts.

“Exactly!” Ms. Raffeli smiles.

And I’m left wondering how I’ll break the news to Mom and Dad that I am now Johanna Quaas, the 86-year-old woman who holds the record for oldest gymnast in the world.

GLITTER AND GLUE STICKS

“We will spend the rest of the day doing an art project.”

"YES!" The Destructor pops out of Ms. Raffeli's lap. "I love art."

"You could go to kindergarten," I say. "They do a lot of art there."

The Destructor ignores me. Ms. Raffeli hands each of us a shoe box, even The Destructor.

"You will fill these boxes with your memories from this school year," she says. "You can use words, drawings, even clay." She points to the center table, where she's put out a bunch of supplies like markers, glue sticks, colored paper, and scissors. "The only rule is that everything must connect to something you have done, either in or out of school this year." She pauses, looks around, and says, "Let's get to work."

And we all do. Ms. Raffeli lets The Destructor sit at Lonnie's seat because both he and Viva and a couple of other students go off to meet their buddies down in kindergarten.

After twenty minutes, The Destructor has a giant mess of marker on his face, glitter in his hair, and glue everywhere else.

Ms. Raffeli leans over me, holding an open container of glitter in each hand. "At least it's all on him," she says just as she walks past me and

slips on glue sticks The Destructor dumped on the floor.

This explains why I am now covered from head to toe in glitter. If only I hadn't screamed when it happened then my mouth would have been closed instead of open.

In *The Guinness Book of World Records* there is a record for walking the greatest distance with a milk bottle balanced on the head (80.96 miles). Walking 80.96 miles balancing anything on my head would be hard, but I have to say getting glitter off the tongue is harder.

THE LAST SPARKLE

I'm still working on my tongue and the glitter when Lonnie and Viva come back. They're all smiles and talking about how cute their buddies are. Then the principal announces over the loudspeaker that there will be an all-school assembly to welcome our incoming kindergarteners.

The only thing worse than welcoming The Destructor to my school would be breaking the record for holding 21 live cockroaches in my mouth.

The gym is packed when we arrive. Every single student and every single visiting student is smiling. I'm smiling, too, because I finally wiped the last piece of glitter off my tongue.

TONGUE-TIED

Grades always sit in groups, so the fifth grade is together, the fourth grade is together, all the way down to kindergarten. The only difference today is that the incoming kindergartners sit in the kindergarten section, and their buddies sit with them. Of course, The Destructor refuses to sit with the other kindergartners, so we stay with Ms. Raffeli, who says to The Destructor, "Try not to move." This is good advice, especially for a kid wearing tin cans.

Lonnie gives me a pat on the back.

Viva says, "Good luck." And they both head off to their buddies.

Ms. Johnson, the principal, taps on her microphone. "Welcome to all the children who are visiting today." I don't hear anything else she says because The Destructor immediately hops over to Angus, his tin cans clanging. I stretch out and

try to stop him, but all I grab is a tin can, which only makes more noise. Ms. Raffeli makes the quiet signal, which is why I miss what is going on until Ms. Raffeli taps me on the shoulder, hands me the microphone, and explains that I should stand up and introduce my brother.

All I see are hundreds of eyes on me. My heart beats faster than the wingbeat of the ruby-throated hummingbird (200 beats per second). My face gets hotter than the hottest chili in the world (Smokin Ed's Carolina Reaper). And to top it off, I try to say something but my mouth feels like it just broke the record for eating the most powdered donuts in three minutes (6). I do not feel good.

All of a sudden The Destructor pops up and says, "Hi, I'm Can Boy. I'm Teddy's brother. I want to make it clear, I'm never taking off my tin cans. I don't care what the rules are!" He hands me the microphone and plops down.

I stand there until Ms. Johnson takes the microphone from my hands and says, "Thank you." And then, like the largest scoop of ice cream (3,010 pounds) after a long day in the sun, I melt to the floor.

CAN'T BREATHE

The rest of the assembly is just a bunch of noise to me, but finally it ends, and that's when Mom shows up to collect The Destructor. She's looking happier than I've seen her in years, which couldn't be more opposite from how I feel.

"Thanks." The Destructor waves good-bye. "This was the best day ever."

Lonnie looks at me and says, "This is a time when breathing like Darth Vader would probably help."

I'm sure he's right, but I feel so mad about this day that I can't even breathe. And I'm only half-way through it!

CAT RECORDS PART 3

Right as we come home, Smarty Pants starts meowing at Lonnie, Viva, and me.

"She must be hungry," Lonnie says. No one is home, not Mom or The Destructor or my sisters. I find a note from Mom: *Be back soon. With a surprise!*

Viva smiles. "I love surprises! Do you think it's a thank-you present for being such a good brother today? Maybe cake, or a new world record book?"

Lonnie shakes his head. "You still don't know Teddy's family very well, do you?"

"What's that mean?" Viva asks.

"It means," I say, "that suprises in my family are never good."

Viva sighs. "You're such a pessimist. That's like saying we're never going to break a record, just because we haven't broken one yet."

"You have a point," I say. "Maybe this surprise will be great."

Lonnie says, "Maybe." And then he laughs.

But since we're talking world records, I move the conversation to breaking a Smarty Pants record. "What can we do?"

Lonnie straightens up. "Because all Smarty Pants ever wants is to eat, we should do a food record."

"I love it." Viva pets Smarty Pants. We decide on the most cat food eaten by a cat in one minute.

"Yuck," I say as I open a can.

"The stink." Lonnie holds his nose.

"How does your mom do it?" Viva waves her hand in front of her face.

I think about this for a minute. "After changing the diapers of seven kids, I'm pretty sure she's totally lost her sense of smell."

Lonnie and Viva agree. It's the only logical explanation.

Anyway, we dump five cans of food in front of Smarty Pants and start timing. But after one minute she's barely gotten through any of it, and after two I'm pretty sure all she's doing is pretending to lick it. After three minutes, she's still working on her food, so we give up.

THE SURPRISE

Lonnie, Viva, and I are about to visit the aviary and think up more Smarty Pants records to break when the front door opens. I hear Mom's voice: "Let me take that for you."

Then a small, white fur ball charges into the kitchen. It runs straight for me and pounces on my feet. Yapping at my shoes, it reaches out and snaps at one of my laces, tugging on the lace with razor-sharp teeth. I'm forced to balance on one foot as it snarls and shakes my lace back and forth like it's about to kill it.

"What's that?" Viva asks.

Lonnie says, "A mad Wookiee?"

It's clearly a dog, but just barely. We've never owned a dog. We're cat people. And speaking of cats, I look around for Smarty Pants and find her hissing in her cat box.

"Would somebody help?" I ask as the dog drags me across the kitchen.

Lonnie backs away. "Not me."

Viva follows Lonnie. "Look at those teeth!"

"Peanut," a voice from the hallway calls. I'd recognize that voice anywhere.

Proving once again that in my family, surprises are always bad.

EVERYTHING CHANGES

"Peanut!" Aunt Ursula squeals. "Come to Mama." She reaches down, but Peanut doesn't come.

Mom leans over the lady, who is blocking the door. "Teddy, you remember Aunt Ursula. And this is her dog, Peanut."

When Peanut hears his name he whips his head back and forth, growls, and tugs harder on my shoelace.

"Teddy, stop moving," Aunt Ursula says. "Peanut is very sensitive. You're scaring him." That is hard to believe.

The Destructor peeks from between Aunt Ursula's legs. "Isn't he adorable?"

Aunt Ursula clucks at Peanut, who finally drops my shoelace.

I try to move away, but Peanut erupts in barking. "Rrrr-ar! Rar-rar-rar!"

"Peanut, come here!" she singsongs to him, but Peanut isn't listening. "Peanut, come here," Aunt Ursula says again.

"Rrrr-ar! Rar-rar-rar!"

Mom says, "You remember Teddy's friend Lonnie."

"Of course I remember Lonnie. You still like Star Wars?"

Lonnie nods.

"Good."

"And that's Viva, another friend." Mom points.

Viva waves.

"Rrrr-ar! Rar-rar-rar!"

"It would be best to stay still," Aunt Ursula says. Viva freezes. Aunt Ursula reaches into her pocket and brings out a treat. "Peanut, come to Mama." Peanut immediately runs for it.

I have three thoughts about this:

1. Why didn't she offer the dog treat right away?
2. What the heck is she doing here so soon?
3. How can everything change so quickly?

NOTHING HAS CHANGED

Peanut jumps into Aunt Ursula's arms and gives her a million kisses. Depending on how you feel

about dog kisses, this is either adorable or gross.

The Destructor takes Aunt Ursula's hand. "This is the trash can I was telling you about. And this is where I like to sort it." He spreads his arms out like he is showing off the record for most expensive bathroom, worth $3.5 million. "Right here on the floor is where I do the sorting. Paper, plastic, and all the other stuff."

"In the kitchen?" Aunt Ursula pulls Peanut a little closer.

The Destructor presses his face against Peanut's and says, "Isn't Peanut the cutest?"

"Mom!" Grace yells from the front door as she slams it. "I'm home!" Right away, Peanut begins his rrar-rar-raring. Grace walks in with her camera already raised to her face. "What's the commotion?" she asks, and clicks away.

"Grace, you remember Aunt Ursula," Mom says.

Grace stops clicking. Her camera slowly moves away from her face. "Nice to see you—" she says, but Peanut, who is still cradled in Aunt Ursula's arms, explodes into more barking.

"RRAR! RRAR! RRAR! RRAR!"

Grace steps back. The first time I've ever seen her do that.

"Now, now, Peanut," Aunt Ursula coos.

The Destructor says, "I don't think Peanut likes you, Grace."

"Peanut doesn't like his picture taken, do you, Peanut?"

Grace looks shocked. She starts to hold up her camera and Peanut starts barking again. That's when Maggie runs into the house dripping with sweat and stink.

"Maggie," Mom says, "Aunt Ursula has arrived early."

Maggie goes to hug her. This time, Aunt Ursula steps back just as Caitlin and Casey bound into the kitchen, laughing their heads off, carrying their bicycle chains, and covered in grease. They freeze. "Aunt Ursula," they say at the exact same time.

Aunt Ursula nods at Casey. "Hello, Caitlin." She nods at Caitlin. "Casey." No one corrects her, which is probably because Sharon's singing pierces the momentary calm.

"Morrrrrning has brooooooken like the first mor-or-or—" She stops at the kitchen door. "Aunt Ursula!"

"Well, this family hasn't changed a bit," Aunt Ursula says, right as Peanut leaps from her arms, dashes over to me, lifts a leg, and pees on my foot.

Aunt Ursula shakes her head. "I told you he was sensitive."

RULES FOR DOGS

1. Dogs should not growl or bark.
2. Dogs should be bigger than a loaf of bread.
3. Dogs should not pee on anyone.

WHAT'S THE RULE?

There are some things that animals do that are cool, like Bertie, the fastest tortoise (0.92 feet per second) or Happie, the record holder for the farthest distance to skateboard by a goat (118 feet). A dog peeing on my leg is not on that list.

But I have to say, for the first time in my life my sisters are absolutely quiet. Grace doesn't even make a peep.

Aunt Ursula grabs Peanut. She looks at Mom. "This was not what I expected."

"Really?" Viva asks out of the corner of her mouth so only Lonnie and I can hear. "Compared to the usual stuff that goes on here, this seems pretty tame."

Lonnie whispers, "Compared to Peanut, Teddy's family seems pretty tame."

Aunt Ursula sighs. "I'll be going now."

Mom reaches out to block her. "You can't leave."

"Leaving? No, I am here as long as you need me." She looks around at all of us. "And you definitely need me. But it's four thirty, which means it's time for one of my favorite rules."

"What's the rule?" The Destructor asks.

"Every day at four thirty is nap time."

The Destructor looks at me. "You didn't tell me she had a nap rule."

"I've taken naps for years, and look how healthy I am." She looks at Mom. "You could use a nap."

I hate to say it, but Aunt Ursula is right, Mom could use a nap.

Aunt Ursula kisses Peanut. "You need a nap, too." She walks out, chatting to Peanut about how tired he looks.

You can tell we're all in shock because even though there's a crowd in the kitchen no one speaks except The Destructor, who says, "I'm still confused about the nap rule."

Mom takes a deep breath, looks at all of us, and says, "I didn't know she was coming. I would have told you, but she surprised me, too."

All of a sudden, Aunt Ursula pops back in. She's still carrying Peanut but now he's got something wrapped around his bottom half.

"Peanut wears a diaper?" The Destructor blurts out. "That's so cool!"

"Only when he sleeps," Aunt Ursula explains. "It's a rule—better safe than sorry."

I have to admit, that seems like a pretty smart rule, for dogs like Peanut or for brothers like The Destructor.

Aunt Ursula looks at Mom. "I'm sure you remember, but I eat dinner at seven."

Mom says, "That's a little late for us."

"No it isn't," Aunt Ursula corrects her. "It's perfectly normal." And she leaves.

Mom smiles. "It's all going to be fine. I know it will. We just have to try to be a little more normal." And then she looks at me. "Let's start with your shoes. I can smell pee."

Sure, Mom can start with my shoes, but it won't get her far. She doesn't know how hard being normal is. It's definitely harder than breaking a world record.

RULES FOR BEING NORMAL

If we want to be normal there's a lot we would have to change.

1. Stop hanging out with pigeons.
2. Get rid of my little brother.
3. Get rid of all my sisters.
4. Stop breaking world records.

In other words, it's impossible.

QUIET TIME

Lonnie and Viva decide that under the circumstances it's probably best that they go home. When I get back from washing my sneaker, sock, and foot, my sisters have all cleared out and Mom is talking to The Destructor about taking a nap.

"Yuck," he says. "Sounds boring."

"We could turn it into a game," she says. "We could see who can be quiet the longest."

I don't wait around to see what he'll decide but leave for the aviary, my own kind of quiet time.

RARE

I sit around watching the pigeons eat and counting the seconds until I get to six hundred and need to take their food away. I'm on 591 when Grumpy Pigeon Man walks into the aviary. I haven't seen him for a few days, so he doesn't know any of my family's news.

"Finally," I say. "Five hundred ninety-two. If I didn't see you today I would have checked to see if you were still alive. Five hundred ninety-three."

"I don't need a babysitter, Tent Boy," he says. "I just had a cold."

I don't take what he says personally because that's just the way he talks. "Five hundred ninety-four. Mom got a job as an animal control officer. Five hundred ninety-five."

"Animal control officer?" He frowns.

"Five hundred ninety-six," I say.

"How are you going to survive without her?"

"Five hundred ninety-seven. My great-aunt Ursula has moved in. Five hundred ninety-eight."

"Is that the same Aunt Ursula who stayed with you before?" He looks over at our house and tucks in his shirt.

"Five hundred ninety-nine. Yup."

"If I remember correctly, she's the one with a lot of rules."

"Six hundred!" I take the food away. "Thank goodness for your pigeons. I don't know what I'd do without them."

Strange but true, there is a category in *The Guinness Book of World Records* for rarest things, like the rarest snake (Antiguan racer), the rarest stamp (a British Guiana One-Cent Magenta from 1856), and the rarest sloth (the pygmy three-toed sloth), but even rarer is Grumpy Pigeon Man smiling, which is what he is doing this very second. I guess it's nice for him to know how much I love his birds.

A NUMBER OF THINGS

I'm back in the kitchen flipping through *The Guinness Book of World Records* when I hear Aunt Ursula come out of the guest room and walk into the bathroom.

Mom and The Destructor come down the stairs.

"I am never doing that again," The Destructor declares.

Mom yawns. "Well, I liked it. And to say thank you for trying it, I have a little something for you. I was going to give it to you later."

I wonder if she got something for me, too. Just like Viva said she might. But Mom holds up a small metal bucket by its handle, and hands it to The Destructor.

The Destructor takes the bucket from her. He lifts the lid on and off. He looks inside. It's empty.

"It's for food scraps," Mom says.

"You mean for compost?"

Mom nods and The Destructor gives Mom a hug and goes straight to the trash and starts digging. He pulls out a banana peel, orange slices, and coffee grinds. Of course, along the way he also dumps all the other trash on the floor. I wonder how Mom connects this to being normal.

And that's when Aunt Ursula walks into the room. Peanut locks eyes with me and growls. He is diaper-free. Aunt Ursula is about to say something, probably some rule she has about compost, but The Destructor holds up his new bucket. "We put food in here and it makes dirt. That's crazy, right? Food becomes dirt!"

He takes a quick breath and keeps talking. "My family is not good about composting yet, but they will be. It's all about learning new ways of doing things. And learning takes time. At least that's what Dad told me yesterday when I was talking to him about how scared I was about you living with us. He says I don't have to worry that you like to do things your way, because you'll learn new ways by living with us. I sure hope so, because quiet time was not much fun. And if that's a rule, I'll probably break it."

The Destructor stops talking and smiles.

And there's a long silence that is intensified by Mom turning bright red.

RULES ABOUT TALKING TO GROWN-UPS

1. Keep it short.
2. Don't tell them everything on your mind.
3. They get hurt feelings about the weirdest things. (Like when I told Mom how she had a hair growing out of her nose that might be able to break a record. I meant it as a compliment; she didn't take it that way at all.)

DINNER

Aunt Ursula cooked dinner tonight. This worries me. Dad's cooking is not good, and Aunt Ursula is from his side of the family. She brings it out and I can honestly say it looks as bad as Dad's, which is not surprising because stuff like this is passed down in families. Just like the Flying Wallendas, who broke the world record for the highest eight-person pyramid on a tightrope and also have been circus performers for seven generations.

Also, it's safe to say that if her cooking is anything like her rules, it's going to be worse than Dad's, because before we even take a bite, Aunt Ursula announces the rules for dinner.

1. Sharon: No singing. (Dinner is a time for conversation.)
2. Casey and Caitlin: No talking about trash. (Dinner is a time for conversation but not about trash.)
3. Maggie: No sit-ups between bites of food. (It causes indigestion.)
4. Grace: No pictures during. (Dinner is a time when we shouldn't have to worry about how we look.)
5. Teddy: No sitting next to Aunt Ursula because of my strange smell. (She doesn't know what the smell is, but she can't stand it.)

She hasn't made a rule about The Destructor eating under the table because Mom and Dad had a whispered conversation about how Jake needed time to adjust to the change and that for tonight it was best to leave him where he was.

Clearly, none of her rules include no dogs at the table, which is why Peanut is sitting in her lap staring ferociously at all of us until Aunt Ursula offers him a bite from her plate and invites us all to start.

The Destructor is the first to try. "This is great!" he says, sticking his head out from under the table. "Almost as good as Dad's."

I still don't try it, remembering that this is coming from The Destructor, and when have I ever agreed with him?

Sharon says, "Wow."

Caitlin and Casey nod.

And Maggie smiles.

Grace is still chewing when she sneaks her camera out and takes a picture. Aunt Ursula is about to get mad but Grace explains, "I need to record the best meal I've ever had."

Aunt Ursula blushes.

So I finally taste it. It's amazing. I never knew food could taste like this. I knew ice cream and candy could, but not regular food.

Maybe having Aunt Ursula around won't be so bad.

WHERE WOULD WE BE WITHOUT RULES?

Before going to bed, Aunt Ursula directs the family into the living room. "If we are to get along while I'm here, I need to explain a few things," she says, pacing back and forth. "Rules are the centerpiece of a society. They guide us. They steer us. They are our lighthouse and our boat." She smiles. "Where would we be without rules? Nowhere." Peanut barks as if he agrees. "Rules create order out of the mayhem of life."

The Destructor raises his hand. "What's 'mayhem of life' mean?"

"Chaos," Grace says, but is cut off by Peanut barking at her, so she whispers the rest. "Havoc, pandemonium."

The Destructor nods. "What's wrong with mayhem?"

Aunt Ursula ignores him. "This is a big family and big families need a few rules so everything runs smoothly, or, as they say, like a well-oiled machine."

"Who says that?" The Destructor asks.

Again Aunt Ursula ignores him. "For the sake of the family, I have drawn up a list of some rules that we shall now follow." She unrolls a poster-size piece of paper.

Strange but true, in 1797 Andre-Jacques Garnerin became the first person to jump out of a hot air balloon with a parachute. He must have been nervous before he did that, and either wanted to just jump right away and get it over with, or never jump at all.

Waiting for Aunt Ursula to read her list of rules makes me feel like I'm that guy.

AUNT URSULA'S RULES

1. Dinner is eaten at seven o'clock. (Too late if you ask me.)
2. Beds are made immediately after waking. (What if I make it after breakfast?)
3. Chairs are always pushed in. (Then you just have to pull them out again.)
4. Napkins must be used, instead of sleeves. (Why make more laundry?)
5. Every morning drink a glass of prune juice.

(You're joking. Prune juice? Never.)

6. Eat everything on your plate. (As long as you cook it.)
7. If you are asked to do something, you do it. (Depends what it is.)
8. Quiet time is scheduled every afternoon. And is expected to be quiet. (Luckily, I've got the pigeons.)

I'M NOT DONE

I know this because we all stand up to leave and she says, "I'm not done."

We sit down.

"These rules," she says, pointing to the ones she's just presented, "will help this family to be more civilized. But there are three other rules that are essential."

She pulls out a second poster, and I can't help wondering when she had time to make all these posters.

1. Children should be productive.
2. Children should be useful.
3. Children should be calm and quiet.

I don't know what children Aunt Ursula knows, but clearly they are nothing like us!

AUNT URSULA NEEDS HELP

The next morning, as usual, no one is awake when I get back from feeding the pigeons. I'm reading the list of rules Aunt Ursula taped to the fridge and eating toast when she comes in with Peanut cradled in her arms.

"Good morning." I wave. Peanut bursts into barks.

"Oh, Teddy!" She puts her hand to her heart. "You scared me. Do you always get up this early?"

I tell her about feeding the pigeons.

"The pigeons. That's what I've been smelling. Now it makes sense. Horrible."

As Aunt Ursula opens and closes a drawer, I sniff myself. I don't smell pigeons, but if I did smell like pigeons, it wouldn't be horrible. Just like them, it would be sweet.

"I was hoping those birds would be gone." She opens and closes another drawer, and then a cabinet.

"Can I help you?"

"Could you find me the tea?"

There's something about the way she says this that makes me feel so sad for her. I suddenly realize what Aunt Ursula is doing for us, and how she's left her own orderly home, with all her rules, to come live with nine people, which even I know is not easy. And all she wants is a cup of tea, and she can't even find it. She probably drinks one every morning before her prune juice (number five on her list), which my parents have not bought for her yet.

"Sit down," I say. "I'll make it for you." I pull over a chair, climbing up on it and then onto the counter.

"Teddy, your feet are on the counter."

"It's the only way I can reach it. It's a really tall cabinet."

She stands up and adds one more rule onto her list, and then says, "No feet on the counter."

"But number seven is if you're asked to do something, do it."

"Technically, I didn't ask you," Aunt Ursula says. "But fine. After this one time, we will find a new place for the tea."

I grab as many different teas as we have and pass them down to her.

And then, still standing on the counter, I pick the prettiest teacup and saucer, because she's the kind of person who would like that. I hop down.

Peanut barks again. "Shh, Peanut. He's helping me."

I have to admit, it's nice to hear her say that.

SMARTY PANTS VERSUS PEANUT

"Thank you." Aunt Ursula raises her cup to sip the tea. Strange but true, I suddenly feel like everything will be all right, which must be how Kevin Shelley felt when he broke 46 toilet seats with his head in one minute and survived. I smile and settle into my seat just as Smarty Pants walks into the room.

Peanut takes one look at Smarty Pants and growls. Smarty Pants takes one look at Peanut and hisses.

Aunt Ursula says, "Peanut usually loves cats."

"Really?" I ask. "Peanut doesn't seem to love anything but you." Suddenly Peanut propels himself out of Aunt Ursula's arms and straight at Smarty Pants. Smarty Pants leaps out of the way, but Peanut is close behind.

Smarty Pants tears past me and bounds up onto the kitchen table, with Peanut following. Smarty Pants knocks over the tea, which spills down Aunt Ursula's nightgown. Peanut runs through my toast as Smarty Pants leaps on top of the fridge. Peanut, who cannot jump that high, is left popping up in the air like he's trying to break the record for most pogo-stick jumps in one minute (266).

Aunt Ursula scoops up Peanut. "There should be a rule about cats," she says.

I admit, I'm sorry that our lovely moment passed so quickly, but for some reason I'm not surprised.

DON'T EVEN ASK

After that hectic morning, I'm happy to be at school working on my memory box. Lonnie, Viva, and I are all working with clay. I'm putting the finishing touches on the dog I made to represent the inventor's fair project we did this year. Lonnie is making Yoda. Viva has finished our lunch table and the trash cans and is working on models of us three. She's already done me, and I can say I'm not looking so good. When I ask her why I'm covered in dripping white stuff, she says, "It's so I can remember all the times you got pooed on by the pigeons."

I make a face. "Couldn't you make me holding a *Guinness Book of World Records*?"

"Too boring."

"Hey, how did the first day with Aunt Ursula go?" Lonnie asks.

"Complicated," I say.

Viva looks up. "How?"

"She's nice, but she doesn't like anything—when we eat, what we drink, when we go to bed—she doesn't even like Smarty Pants."

"She must like something," Lonnie says

I place the dog in my memory box. "She

likes rules, naps, and the tea I made for her this morning."

"She likes Peanut." Viva smiles.

I'm quiet for a minute as I think about how anyone could like Peanut!

Lonnie stops drawing. "When does your mom start work?"

"I don't know." Thinking about it makes me feel like the largest orchestra in the world (7,224 musicians) is playing in my stomach.

Then Viva asks, "How about world records? Do you think she likes that?"

"I think sometimes it's best not to even ask," I say. "And this is one of those times."

And we all promise that our rule is that Aunt Ursula will never find out about our record-breaking habit.

STRONGEST FORCE IN THE UNIVERSE

Today, when Lonnie, Viva, and I walk into the kitchen, none of us can believe what we see. The Destructor is sitting at the table. Let me repeat: sitting at the table!

In my book, that comes pretty close to breaking a world record. Peanut is sitting at his feet.

"Guess what?" The Destructor asks. "Never mind, I'll tell you. Peanut likes me!" He reaches down and gives Peanut a treat. Peanut gobbles it up, then looks at me and growls.

"Where's Mom?"

Aunt Ursula walks in. Her face is covered in brown mud. "Hello, Teddy. Oh, you brought your friends over. Excuse my appearance—you're never too old for a little exfoliating—but I thought there would be some rule about asking if guests could come over."

The Destructor shakes his head. "Lonnie and Viva aren't guests. They're more like cousins."

"Where's Mom?" I repeat.

"She had a training to go to before she starts her job," Aunt Ursula says.

My heart sinks as I'm reminded of life without Mom. When will I ever see her?

Then I look at The Destructor. He's still sitting in the chair. If Mom is away at a training then that means Aunt Ursula did that.

I lean over to her and whisper, "How'd you get him to sit at the table?"

"My little secret," she whispers back. "Next, we'll get him out of his tin cans." And she smiles.

In *The Guinness Book of World Records* they explain that there are four fundamental forces in the universe: gravitational, electromagnetic, weak nuclear, and strong nuclear. Out of those four, the most powerful is strong nuclear. In fact, it's the force that holds atoms together.

If Aunt Ursula could get The Destructor out of his tin cans, she would definitely beat that record to become the most powerful force in the universe.

I pause to think about this, then burst out laughing.

There's no way she can ever be that strong.

CUPCAKES

"I understand you're hungry when you get home." She takes down a plate full of cupcakes.

"Aren't they funny-looking?" The Destructor says. The cupcakes look like bugs. Each one is green and has lots of eyes made out of icing and antennae made from cucumber peels.

Aunt Ursula smiles and the mud on her face starts to crumble. "One of my rules: if you're going to do something, then do it right."

"That's a great rule!" The Destructor says.

If last night's dinner is anything to go on, these should be delicious, but there's always the chance that was just a fluke, and everything else she makes will be as bad as Dad's.

"Help yourself," Aunt Ursula says. "I'm going to wash the mud off my face."

"Can I watch?" The Destructor asks. He follows Aunt Ursula, who carries Peanut over her shoulder.

Lonnie and Viva grab a cupcake. I wait for them to take bites. Their mouths spread out in huge grins, and then I grab one, too. It's chocolaty and delicious, and totally the best cupcake I've ever had.

Viva says, "If this is what life with Aunt Ursula will be like, maybe you should stop complaining."

"I don't know," I say.

Lonnie says, "In the words of Yoda, 'You will find only what you bring in.' So maybe you want to be a little more positive and see how it goes."

Lonnie has a point. And knowing Lonnie the way I do, I know I should listen to him, but it's not as easy as it sounds.

RECORDS WE WOULD NEVER DO

Aunt Ursula convinces The Destructor to have quiet time by saying he can help put Peanut's diaper on.

"I'll give it one more chance," he says, "but only because of the diaper."

Aunt Ursula reminds us to keep our voices down.

"That won't be hard," I say. "We'll be reading."

After they're gone, I pull out *The Guinness*

Book of World Records. We're looking for a record we could break but for some reason we only notice the entries that are too impossible, too dangerous, or just too gross.

Records like:

1. Highest forward flip jump on a pogo stick (9 feet 2 inches).
2. Most coconuts smashed with the elbows in one minute (40).
3. Smallest waist ever (13 inches).
4. Largest playing-card structure (34 feet 1.05 inches long, 9 feet 5.39 inches tall, and 11 feet 7.37 inches wide).
5. Largest number of cockroaches in a coffin (John Lamedica climbed into a coffin with 20,050 cockroaches).
6. Largest scorpion held in the mouth (7 inches long).

This last one really gets to Lonnie, Viva, and me. I mean, putting a scorpion in your mouth is bad enough, but the guy kept it there for eighteen seconds!

If that's what you have to do to break a record then the three of us are seriously in trouble.

THAT'S WHEN I SEE IT

Just when I'm about to get discouraged, I find the perfect record. It's so exciting that it's hard to stay quiet, but I don't want to wake up Aunt Ursula. So I point and whisper, "Most scoops of ice cream thrown and caught in one minute by a team of two."

"But we're three people," Viva whispers back.

"So what?" I shrug. "We'll be a team of three people."

"They tossed and caught twenty-five scoops," Lonnie reads quietly.

Viva opens the freezer. "You certainly have got enough ice cream."

"There's more in the basement," I say. In my family, we buy everything in bulk.

Personally, I don't like going down into the basement anymore, and it's not because of the cobwebs; they've always been there. Last month, I went up and down about a million times hiding plastic bags. But it all changed when Grace told me about the zombie that lives down there. She thought this was hilarious, and added a lot of details that I will not repeat.

For the record, I didn't think it was hilarious,

and even after Mom and Dad took me down to prove that the whole thing was made up, it didn't matter; the story was stuck in my head, and once it's stuck, there's no getting it unstuck.

"What will we use?" Lonnie asks, only finding one ice-cream scoop.

I grab a spatula, a ladle, and the ice cream.

Lonnie says, "Remember, we've got to be quiet."

Viva nods.

And I think, this is the best record ever. Nothing could go wrong.

NOT LIKE I PLANNED

Let me start by saying we were really on a roll. Lonnie threw to Viva. Viva threw to me. I threw to Lonnie. We had thrown and caught six scoops of ice cream, which is really good, considering we were using an ice-cream scoop, a spatula, and a ladle.

And then I missed a catch and got thwacked in the face with mint chocolate chip.

Because Lonnie was so focused, he didn't see it happen, but Viva did, and because she did, she looked away from Lonnie, and because she looked away from Lonnie, she got a scoop of ice cream in her face.

Luckily, that's when Lonnie looked up.

And that's when we all started laughing, because throwing and catching ice cream is funny, but not catching it is funnier, even if it means we don't break a record.

I looked at Lonnie and his ice-cream-free face, and clearly, there is only one thing to do.

I scoop out a spatula-ful and throw it. Right at Lonnie, but at that exact moment Lonnie doubles over from laughing so hard, and Aunt Ursula

walks in, and the ice cream flies over Lonnie's laughing body and lands on Aunt Ursula's face.

If my rule is that Aunt Ursula would never find out about the world records, I can honestly say I have failed.

On the other hand, we might have broken the record for fastest rule to ever be broken.

LUCKILY AND UNLUCKILY

Luckily, Mom sweeps in right then, looks around, gasps, and hustles Aunt Ursula off to the bathroom.

Peanut is forgotten and he runs around the kitchen licking up the ice cream that has dripped everywhere. And even though Lonnie, Viva, and I try to catch him, it's no good. He scoots around us, licking all the way.

There's lot of stuff I don't know. That's one of the reasons I love *The Guinness Book of World Records*. But a few things I didn't know that are not in the book are that some dogs shouldn't eat ice cream.

Unluckily, if some dogs eat ice cream they get diarrhea, or the runs, as Dad calls it.

Extremely unluckily, Peanut is one of these dogs.

PEANUT VERSUS PIGEONS

Usually, Grumpy Pigeon Man never comes out in the morning, and if he does, he's in his pajamas. But this morning, he does come out. And he's dressed and everything. He's even wearing a tie.

He nods to me.

"Three hundred eighty-seven," I say.

He picks up a bucket, flips it over, and sits down.

"Three hundred eighty-eight. You going somewhere fancy?" I ask. He is wearing a tie, after all.

"Nope," he says.

"Three hundred eighty-nine."

"How's your family?"

"Pretty good. Three hundred ninety." I don't bother telling him about the ice-cream fiasco yesterday.

"Has your mom started working?"

"Soon," I say. "Three hundred ninety-one."

He clears his throat. "How's Ursula?"

"Three hundred ninety-two. You mean Aunt Ursula?"

He clears his throat again.

"She's okay, I guess. Three hundred ninety-three. She got The Destructor sitting in a chair. Three hundred ninety-four."

"I haven't seen her yet."

"Three hundred ninety-five. She's pretty busy. She has a—"

Right then there's an explosion of barking. And a blur of white streaks across my backyard and up to the aviary. The pigeons fly up, and even though there's a fence between our yards, and the pigeons are closed in safe and sound, they try to get as far away from the barking as possible.

Grumpy Pigeon Man leaps up and stares through the screen. "What the pigeon feathers is that?"

GRUMPY PIGEON MAN VERSUS PEANUT

"It's Peanut," I say. "Four hundred five."

"It's a barking rat!"

"Rats don't bark. Four hundred six."

"This rat barks!" Grumpy Pigeon Man yells. "It's a world record, Teddy. The first ever barking rat!"

And the whole time that Grumpy Pigeon Man is yelling, Peanut is barking, which makes me think they have more in common than they know.

"No, it's a dog. Aunt Ursula has a dog."

Grumpy Pigeon Man looks surprised. He frowns and says, "I think you should take the food away now." I didn't realize I stopped counting. I do what Grumpy Pigeon Man suggests, which ought to make Aunt Ursula happy since one of her rules is to do what people ask you to do.

Peanut is still jumping around the fence, digging in the dirt, and barking his little body off, while Grumpy Pigeon Man has gotten very still.

GRUMPY PIGEON MAN VERSUS AUNT URSULA

"Peanut!" Aunt Ursula calls from our back door. Peanut is doing an excellent job ignoring her.

"She hasn't changed a bit." Grumpy Pigeon Man sighs and leaves the aviary. I figure he's heading back into his house, but then I see him walk into our backyard. He scoops up Peanut, who stops barking right away, and brings him to Aunt Ursula.

I close up the aviary and run over after him. I have no idea what I'll find, but I'm pretty sure I do not want to miss it.

Aunt Ursula is now hugging Peanut. "How could you say that about Peanut? He's gentler than your pigeons!"

"What?" Grumpy Pigeon Man huffs. "My pigeons wouldn't hurt a fly."

"My dog is simply protecting me from your birds." She takes a deep breath and then says, "You shouldn't be allowed to keep them!"

Strange but true, there's a record for most toilet plungers thrown and stuck to human targets in one minute (15). The look of shock on Grumpy Pigeon Man's face is like all 15 have hit him.

"Keep that dog inside where he can't disturb my birds," he says.

"My dog has as much right to be outside as your birds. There is no rule against it!"

They stare into each other's eyes for a few seconds and then Grumpy Pigeon Man walks away.

"There should be a rule about being so stubborn," Aunt Ursula grumbles as we walk back to the house.

I can't help thinking there should be a rule about grown-ups fighting, but since grown-ups make the rules, the chances of that happening are small.

RULES ABOUT JUICE

1. It needs to be prune juice.
2. It needs to be drunk in the morning.
3. It needs to be put on the grocery list or life will be bad for all of us. (Not just for me, who happens to be the only one awake with Aunt Ursula in the mornings.)

LITTLE BLOBS OF CLAY

Between Mom going back to work, Aunt Ursula moving in, and the end of school, my brain is mush. This is probably why I'm just making little blobs with the clay. Meanwhile Viva seems fine and at this moment is drawing a picture of me covered in pigeons. I have to say, I like it a lot more than me covered in pigeon poo. Lonnie is adding a light saber to his clay Yoda, and except for the fact that every time he lets go, Yoda tips over, he's fine, too.

Ms. Raffeli walks past. "Teddy? What are those?"

I think fast and say, "Pigeon bodies." I pick up one and smoosh a beak on it.

"Well, remember, there's only a few days left, and that's a lot of pigeons."

"Fifty-seven. I've only made—" I count them and get to twenty before Serena calls for help because a bottle of glitter glue spilled in her hair.

I go back to making my blobs because it's all my brain can handle.

ZOMBIES ON DAGOBAH

After school, Lonnie and Viva come over. We've already promised Mom we'll stay outside whenever we try to break a record.

Mom says, "Aunt Ursula will get her nap, and it will be quiet in our house. Do you understand?"

We all nod.

The only way The Destructor agrees on quiet time is when Aunt Ursula says he can help with Peanut's diaper again. After that, he gives her a big hug and heads upstairs with Mom.

Lonnie, Viva, and I sit in the aviary flipping through *The Guinness Book of World Records.*

Lonnie stops at a record and points.

The tallest toilet-paper tower that's ever been built in 30 seconds is 28 rolls high. Some families might not have that much toilet paper, but my family does, so I am sure we have enough to beat this record. The only challenge is going down to the basement, where it's kept, but for a world record, I'll do it.

"Don't make a sound," I whisper as I open the back door.

"Wasn't planning on it," Viva whispers.

"My mind is as quiet as if I were a Jedi." Lonnie closes the door without a sound.

We tiptoe into the house. We sneak past the guest room, where little snores are coming from. I can't tell if it's Aunt Ursula or Peanut who's doing the snoring, but it's cute either way.

We get to the top of the basement stairs. I take a breath and then head down. Even with the lights on I'm sure I can see a zombie hiding behind a trunk.

Lonnie whistles. "The resemblance to Dagobah is uncanny."

"Dagobah?" I ask, passing an old Halloween costume of a skeleton.

"You know, the swamp where Yoda lived."

Viva shudders. "I'd rather live in Dagobah any day."

"Me too," I say.

We grab all the toilet-paper rolls and run upstairs as fast as we can. We pound into the kitchen, terrified. But I guess we don't do a good job on the quiet part because Aunt Ursula calls out, "What's going on?"

"Sorry," I say, and tiptoe out the back door before she asks us any more questions.

We count the rolls and get to twenty-six.

"We'll need more," Lonnie says.

"We took everything from the basement," I say.

"Time to plunder the bathrooms," Viva whispers, like she's a very quiet pirate.

"Arr, matey, but what if someone needs toilet paper?" Lonnie asks back in more quiet pirate speak.

Viva drops the pirate speak and looks at us very seriously. "We survived the basement, and zombies, and even Aunt Ursula." Viva shrugs. "Someone needing toilet paper is a risk we'll have to take."

She's got a point, and what are the chances anyone is going to need toilet paper right when we're breaking a record?

I mean, most of my family isn't even home and the rest are asleep. We'll definitely be done before anyone needs the toilet.

THE FIRST FOUR TIMES

Going back into the house and collecting all the toilet paper is the easy part. Breaking the toilet paper tower record is another story.

1. The first time we forgot to turn on the timer.
2. The second time we forgot chairs, so we couldn't reach the top as we added rolls.
3. The third time we needed something firmer than grass to put the rolls on because they tipped over.
4. The fourth time we needed to put the rolls on something flat instead of the hill in my backyard where we had started.

LARGEST LAND CRAB

Now we're on the fifth try and I actually think we're going to break it.

We're working like a machine, taking turns placing the toilet-paper rolls on top of each other. We start on the ground, and then move to standing on chairs. Our timing is perfect. Our placement is perfect.

"Eleven," I say, placing it on the tower.

"We're doing great." Viva puts number twelve on.

"Lucky number thirteen," Lonnie says.

"We got this," I add.

“The Force is with us.” Lonnie sets the sixteenth roll on the tower, when a scream erupts from the house, startling me so much that I fall over backward. My feet kick up and topple over our tower.

“Teddy!” Lonnie and Viva sigh.

There’s another scream. We look at each other and run inside, but nothing is happening.

"Who screamed?" Viva asks.

Lonnie looks around. "Maybe Sharon and Jerome came back and are practicing?"

I shake my head. "It sounds too good to be them."

"Help!"

"It's coming from the bathroom," Viva says.

"Do you think it's—" Lonnie doesn't finish his sentence.

"Don't say it."

"Aunt Ursula?" Viva finishes.

"I told you not to say it."

Lonnie pushes me to the door. "Ask her if she's all right."

I look at Lonnie. "I'm not knocking. Aunt Ursula is inside. That's gross."

Viva whispers, "It could be your mom stuck in the bathroom."

And for a second I wonder if it is Mom, but then Aunt Ursula's voice rings out from behind the closed door along with a bunch of barks. Of course she brought Peanut.

"Whoever is there, please pass me some toilet paper!"

Strange but true, the world's largest and heaviest

land crustacean is called the robber crab. It can grow up to 36 inches and weigh as much as 9 pounds.

Instead of helping Aunt Ursula, we do the same thing we'd do if we saw a robber crab. We take a giant step away from the door.

SCARIER THAN THE ZOMBIE BASEMENT

Lonnie and Viva elbow me, jolting my brain back to the present. Aunt Ursula is in the bathroom with no toilet paper. It's not complicated; it's just weird. "One minute Aunt Ursula."

We run outside to grab the toilet paper and stop in our tracks.

"It's raining," Viva says. "When did it start raining?"

"It's raining hard," Lonnie says. "When did it start raining so hard?"

"I don't know," I say. "But I think I just found out what's scarier than the basement."

It's clear from Lonnie's and Viva's faces that they agree and that zombie basement is a million times better than Aunt Ursula in the bathroom without any toilet paper.

ICE-CREAM CAKE

We walk back into the house, dripping all over the floor as we carry the soaking-wet toilet paper.

"What is taking so long?" Aunt Ursula calls from the bathroom. Peanut barks again.

I look at Viva. "You're a girl. You hand it to her."

Viva shakes her head. "No way. This is a job for your mom."

Lonnie nods. "That is the sort of advice that Obi-Wan Kenobi might give."

"I think even Chewie would give it," Viva says.

Aunt Ursula hollers through the door, "What is taking so long?"

I edge my way closer, but when I'm an arm's length away, I stop. "We'll be back. I need to find Mom."

We dump all the wet toilet-paper rolls by the door as Aunt Ursula screams, "Do no such thing!" and "Come back this instant!" and "Stop right now!" We don't listen. We run upstairs.

Mom is fast asleep in the room I share with The Destructor. He's lying on the bed next to her looking at a book about a trash truck.

"Mom." I shake her. "We have a toilet emergency."

She rolls over and says, “I don’t want to wake up.”

And right then another scream travels up from downstairs, all the way through the halls of the house, up the stairs, and into the room we’re in.

“Oh no,” Mom says, and hurries away. The rest of us run after, trying to explain why all the toilet paper in the house is about as absorbant as the largest ice-cream cake in the world (14 feet 7 inches long, 13 feet 3 inches wide, and 3 feet 3 inches tall). In other words, not at all.

At least you could eat the ice-cream cake. There’s nothing you can do with wet toilet paper, not even break a record.

NORMAL

Lonnie and Viva leave right after Mom deals with the wet toilet paper problem. If I were those two, I’d do the same.

“Mom,” I say. “I’m really sorry about the toilet paper. We didn’t know it was going to rain.”

“I know.” She hugs me. “I’ll get Dad to pick some more up.”

“Tell him not to forget the prune juice. It might make up for the toilet paper.”

"But Teddy." Mom smiles. "Could we try a little harder to keep things normal around here?"

Considering that things have never been normal, it seems a lot to ask, but I nod because I can tell that's what Mom needs, which is when Aunt Ursula walks into the kitchen.

She is carrying Peanut, who growls at me and then at Smarty Pants. Smarty Pants hisses and jumps on top of the refrigerator.

"Well, I wasn't sure I'd ever get out of there. Would someone explain why all the toilet paper is wet? Is there a leak?"

Mom and I look at each other. But before we have to answer, The Destructor walks in. "Why didn't anyone tell me quiet time was over?" He doesn't wait for an answer. "Hi, Peanut! Did you have a good nap?"

He scratches Peanut's belly. "Aunt Ursula, did you know I'm very good with animals? Mr. Marney can tell you. I helped take care of his pigeons, except I stopped. It's very tiring." He kisses Peanut's nose, and Peanut licks his face.

"Pigeons." Aunt Ursula makes a face like she just beat the record for drinking a liter of lemon juice through a straw in 24.41 seconds. "Why someone hasn't gotten rid of them is a mystery to me."

Now it's my turn to make a face. Life without those pigeons would be like a life without world records.

Peanut jumps out of Aunt Ursula's arms and runs straight at me. I freeze.

Aunt Ursula looks at Mom. "You shouldn't let your children take care of them. It's not normal."

"Oh!" The Destructor interrupts, pointing at Peanut, who is lifting his leg and once again pees on my sneaker.

"Oops! Silly Peanut."

I have to say, I'm having a hard time figuring out what counts as normal around here.

RULES FOR BEING NORMAL PART 2

1. Don't talk about world records.
2. Don't talk about pigeons.
3. Don't try to understand what is normal to grown-ups, because it doesn't make any sense.

DINNER AT VIVA'S HOUSE

You can tell my family is willing to put up with a lot to eat Aunt Ursula's dinner because tonight we follow her rules without being asked. I admit, I borrowed some of Mom's perfume so I won't smell like pigeons. Mom and Dad locked Smarty Pants in their room. And when Aunt Ursula tapped the chair next to hers and said to The Destructor, "Sit," like he was a dog, he did.

For the first time in my life I think I know what dinner is like at Viva's house.

SPINNING TOPS

Dad and I are cleaning up after dinner. Mom is filling out forms for her new job. Aunt Ursula is sitting at the kitchen table doing a crossword puzzle. The Destructor sits on the floor filling up the compost bucket with food scraps. "This is so cool," he says. It looks like a big mess to me.

Grace is taking closeup shots of different parts of our bodies. I wave her away from my nose.

"But it's so gross," she says.

Maggie is doing burpees, and counting each one as she completes it.

Caitlin and Casey wander into the kitchen carrying parts of their bikes and a toolbox. They lay a sheet on the floor and dump everything down with a loud clatter. No one is bothered by them. Dad walks over them to put away a pan. Mom hands them a tool, and ends up with oil all over her hands, but she doesn't complain.

Sharon's singing drifts through the house from the upstairs bathroom.

Aunt Ursula frowns. "It's hard to do a crossword with all this commotion."

Dad says, "You'll get used to it."

Am I the only one who doesn't see Aunt Ursula getting used to us?

Strange but true, the world record for most simultaneous spinning tops is 27. I feel like Aunt Ursula's brain is spinning around and around like all those tops.

I can't help wondering what she'll do when they stop.

IT WON'T HELP

"So do we have two or three days left of school?" Viva asks as we stand in line for school. "I can't keep it straight."

Angus hops over. "One and a half."

Lonnie shakes his head. "Two and a half," he says. "We're just starting today and it's Thursday."

Ny shakes her head. "I can't believe we have to come back on Monday. Who ends school on a Monday?"

Lewis nods. "That's what I was going to say."

Either way I feel really sad. But I'm thinking maybe Ms. Raffeli needs the vacation because her allergies are so bad. She's always wiping her eyes and blowing her nose.

I hand her a tissue. "Why don't you take medicine?"

"It won't help for the kind of allergies I have," she says.

I wonder what kind of allergies she has. "I really think you should breathe like Darth Vader."

I don't know why, but she starts crying more.

MORE SURPRISES

This afternoon, Lonnie and Viva come over and we spend it in the backyard trying to break the record for fastest time to set up a chessboard (32.42 seconds). And even though it's not a team record, it's still a great record to attempt because Aunt Ursula thinks we're playing chess. I see her checking on us.

Viva is flat on the ground laughing her head off as Lonnie tries to get the chess pieces right. He has maybe five or six in the correct spot, the rest have all tipped over, and it's already 25 seconds.

"And time's up!" I shout. Lonnie falls down on the ground, too.

Just then the back door opens and Peanut dashes out. He runs straight at us, barking his little head off. Then he runs to the fence next to

the pigeons and barks at them. Then back to us. Then to the pigeons.

The Destructor wanders outside. "Peanut," he calls. "Come here!" And Peanut does it.

This is surprising, but not as surprising as the fact that The Destructor is not wearing his tin cans.

I stand up. "Hey," I say. "What happened to your tin can coat?"

"I don't wear it anymore," he says. "Aunt Ursula thought Peanut would like me more if I took it off." He scoops up Peanut. "I think she's right."

"Weird," Lonnie says.

"Weird," Viva says.

"Definitely weird," I agree, and then I get worried because if she can do that, what else can she do?

LAST FRIDAY OF FOURTH GRADE

Strange but true, school is like eating the most baked beans one by one with a cocktail stick. It feels like it's going to last forever, that it will never end, and then all of a sudden you've eaten 2,780 baked beans and you've broken a record, or, in this case, school is over.

The only difference is that when you break a world record you're really, really happy.

SHARON'S GRADUATION

Sometimes things happen in my family that I don't even know about until the very day. Sharon's graduation is one of those things, and is why Lonnie and Viva can't come over today. It's Saturday afternoon and the whole family is wearing nicer clothes than usual and piling into the van.

"Peanut can't stay at home alone," Aunt Ursula says as she climbs in with Peanut. "He's too fragile."

I'm pretty sure she's wrong about Peanut being fragile. I'm also pretty sure there's a rule about no dogs allowed at a graduation, but this is one rule Aunt Ursula doesn't seem to care about.

Just as Aunt Ursula thought, no one asks about Peanut. In fact, no one noticed him, not even his growls because of how wonderful Sharon and Jerome sang.

I'm just glad it's over, because if I had to hear that song one more time I might have to break the record for most custard pies in the face in one minute (71). Just to be clear, the faces would have been theirs. I'm pretty sure it could have stopped them from singing.

At least for a few minutes, and sometimes, that's all you can hope for.

TOMORROWS

Usually tomorrows are full of hope and excitement, but right now tomorrow feels about as heavy as the heaviest cabbage (138.25 pounds). Tomorrow is the last day of school and Mom's first day at her new job.

I can tell my sisters feel the same because they are slumped over different pieces of furniture in the living room, doing nothing. I'm sitting on the floor because there isn't anywhere else for me. The Destructor is curled back up inside his cat box, which is a clear sign of how sad he is.

Mom, on the other hand, rushes around putting out clothes for her first day of work, packing her lunch, and collecting pencils and paper as if they won't have them at the animal control office.

"Jake!" Aunt Ursula screams. "Why are you back in that thing? A litter box is only for cats."

"That's what you think."

Just then Dad walks in. He whispers something to Aunt Ursula. She says, "It goes against all the rules for how children should behave."

He whispers some more and she says, "Just this once. But I won't have him living in there. It's not right."

I think the only way to describe the rest of the night is to say that it is sadder than when Ashrita Furman's record for running the fastest mile while wearing swim fins (7 minutes 56 seconds) was broken by someone else (5 minutes and 48.86 seconds).

There's something so sad when a record gets beaten. I know it's part of life, but it's still miserable.

RULES ABOUT SADNESS

1. Don't show the person who's making you sad that you are sad.
2. Don't complain to the person who has come to take care of you that you are sad.
3. I'm too sad to think of any other rules.

MONDAY MORNING

The Destructor clings to Mom's leg like the world's largest leech (18 inches).

"I'll be home before dinner," she says as she tries to peel him off. But like that leech, he's not budging.

"Don't worry, Jake," Dad says. "It's going to be okay." He peels him off as Mom barrels out the door and before she bursts into tears.

I know this because I run out after her to give her the lunch she made and forgot, and also to give her a good luck hug with no one else around. To be honest, I'm crying, too.

My sisters leave for school,

and I'm about to follow them when The Destructor climbs back into the cat box. I say the first thing in my head. "Just breathe like Darth Vader. It really makes you feel better."

The Destructor breathes in and out. "I don't feel any better."

"Lonnie taught me," I say. "Just breathe slowly." I sit with him for a few seconds while we breathe together. "Make the noise. That's important."

"Whhhhhh-whoooh-whhhhh-whoooh." And after a few breaths he actually smiles.

The Destructor peeks his head out of the cat box. "Aunt Ursula, you want to breathe with me?"

Aunt Ursula closes the dishwasher. "Climb out of that thing and I'll go to the moon with you."

The Destructor laughs but doesn't climb out.

"Peanut needs a bath. Want to help?" she asks him.

"Why does Peanut need a bath?" The Destructor asks.

"He's old. Sometimes old dogs need baths."

"But you haven't had him for long."

"I adopted him last year."

"Didn't you want a puppy?"

She smiles. "I wanted Peanut."

The Destructor nods. "That's nice." He climbs out of the cat box and takes Aunt Ursula's hand. They walk out of the room together.

This day is still one of the saddest I've ever known, but that made it just a little bit better.

MONDAY MORNING PART 2

I'm halfway down the block when Aunt Ursula comes trotting after me. I see The Destructor on the steps holding Peanut. "Teddy!" she calls. "Teddy, wait!" She's way more athletic than I thought.

I stop.

"I meant to give this to you." She hands me a form with my parents' and her signatures and The Destructor's and my names printed on it.

"What's this?" I ask.

"For the mural project. I've signed you two up."

"W-what?" I stammer. "I never do anything in the summer."

"I'm sorry I didn't tell you, but it is a rule of mine: when we can, we do for others. The mural project is a wonderful opportunity to do something for your community."

Strange but true, the fastest time to solve a Rubik's cube while juggling is 22.25 seconds. I go from thinking Aunt Ursula is the best to the worst faster than that. To top it off it feels like I'm juggling and solving at the same time.

I guarantee you, that is too much for a ten-year-old kid.

THE MURAL PROJECT

By the time I get to school, my grade has already gone inside, so I walk straight into the classroom. I walk past Lonnie, Viva, Ny, and Angus and I don't say hello. In fact, I don't stop until I hand Ms. Raffeli the form.

"You are signing up?" she asks.

"Aunt Ursula wants me to do it."

Ms. Raffeli smiles. "You never know, you might actually have fun."

"Without Lonnie and Viva?" I ask and then point to the form. "And with my brother?"

Ms. Raffeli's eyebrows rise up as tall as the

highest mountain in the world (Mount Everest, 29,028 feet 9 inches). "You've lived through worse. And the good news is your mom works in the building you'll be painting."

"How'd you know she was working there?" I ask, but before she answers, Lonnie and Viva walk over. They're both holding out permission forms for Ms. Raffeli.

"You're doing it?" I ask.

"I thought I'd be the only one," Lonnie says.

"Me too!" Viva smiles.

We raise our hands to do a three-way high five. Once again we miss our hands and hit our faces. I can only hope that this summer is better than our high fives, or else we'll all be in a lot of trouble.

RULES FOR THE LAST DAY OF SCHOOL

1. Breathe so you don't cry as soon as you have your last morning meeting of fourth grade.
2. Breathe so you don't cry when you clean out your desk and find a card Ms. Raffeli gave you after you broke a world record.
3. Breathe so you don't cry when your friends do stuff that for the whole year drove you crazy but now you think is funny.
4. Breathe so you don't cry when Ms. Raffeli gives you her copy of *The Guinness Book of World Records*, because it's the best present a teacher ever gave you.
5. Breathe so you don't cry when you hand her the card you quickly made when she wasn't looking and you were supposed to be washing your desk.
6. Breathe so you don't cry when it's time to really say good-bye to your teacher after she's given you her copy of *The Guinness Book of World Records* from when she was a kid, because even if you are crying, it's still important to breathe.

A NEW HOBBY

The school year is finished. Done. I've graduated from fourth grade! I walk into the kitchen pretending that Mom will be there, but know she won't. I stop in my tracks. And because of that Lonnie bumps into me, and because he bumps into me, Viva bumps into him.

"We have to stop walking so close," Lonnie says.

"What's the hold up?" Viva asks.

I point to The Destructor, who is sitting at the table with Peanut in his lap. He's not in his cat box, he's not in his tin can coat, he's not under a table, and he's not rooting through trash!

He's sitting quietly, working on some contraption that's laid out in front of him. He's moving a stick in and out of a string. The stick has colored yarn attached.

"Haven't you seen someone weaving before?" The Destructor asks.

To be honest, I've never seen anyone weaving, but that is not why I stopped. I stopped because I've never seen him looking so calm.

He pulls the stick in and out. "Aunt Ursula taught me. She said I needed a new hobby. I'm making a blanket for Peanut!"

"Wow," I say to Aunt Ursula. "Any chance you can teach new hobbies to my sisters?" I actually laugh out loud at that because the thought of my sisters doing anything different cracks me up.

"That's my plan," she says, then hands us each a cupcake.

We gasp. It looks exactly like R2-D2. Aunt Ursula is full of surprises and this is a great one.

Which makes me wonder why I feel so worried?

RULES FOR WHEN YOUR MOM COMES HOME FROM HER FIRST DAY OF WORK

1. Rub Mom's feet because she is tired.
2. Let yourself be pushed off the sofa in the middle of a cuddle because six other siblings want to cuddle, too.
3. Don't fight with your siblings over anything.
4. Be excited for her because it really is amazing to see her so happy.
5. Go to bed when Aunt Ursula says even if it is earlier than usual.

MORE BENEFICIAL

Lonnie and Viva arrive after breakfast. We're all determined to break a record before the end of the summer. If we're going to meet that deadline, we really need to focus.

The Destructor is weaving at the kitchen table. "I'm almost done with Peanut's blanket." He beams.

Lonnie and Viva give him the thumbs-up.

Aunt Ursula is taking oatmeal cookies out of the oven. They smell amazing.

I'm about to grab a few for us and head out to the aviary.

"Before you go," Aunt Ursula says, "could you tell me who these belong to?" She's holding two of my *Guinness Book of World Records* books.

"Uh," I say. "They're mine." I try to take them from her, but she doesn't release them. I can't believe I left them out.

She flips through one. "Juggling chainsaws, collecting rubber ducks—humans should not do these things."

I'm making the universal "let's get out of here" signal with my head, but Viva doesn't see it. "Technically," she says helpfully, "most of the records *are* broken by humans."

I cringe. What is Viva doing? I thought we had a rule about not talking to Aunt Ursula about world records. "Well, the pigeons need their food." I head for the back door.

"Teddy loves breaking world records," The Destructor says. "Maybe it's more like *trying* to break them."

I cringe.

"Really?" Aunt Ursula asks. "Your parents let you do those things?"

"Usually," Lonnie says. I can tell he's trying to be polite. When a grown-up asks you something, you do need to answer.

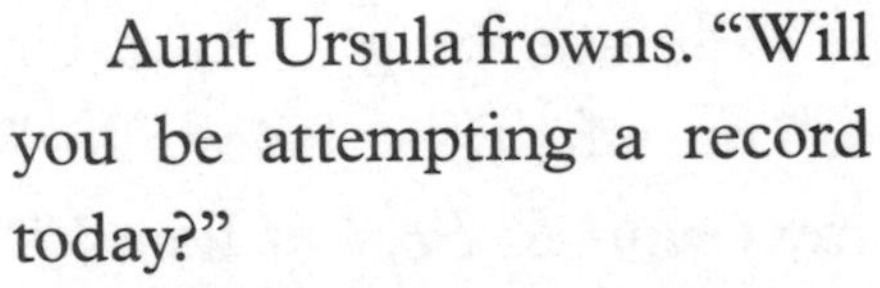

Aunt Ursula frowns. "Will you be attempting a record today?"

We all look at each other.

Aunt Ursula shakes her head. "I don't like that idea. Breaking records doesn't seem right."

Compared to what? I wonder, but keep the question to myself.

"No, my mind is set. You

three can do something much more beneficial with your time. Mowing the lawn, for instance." She looks at me.

"Okay!" I grab Lonnie and Viva. We run out as she shouts, "Today!" We don't even go back for a cookie.

When we're safely in the aviary, Lonnie says, "What's more beneficial than breaking a world record?"

We all shake our heads because none of us can think of anything.

Definitely not mowing a lawn.

WHAT GROWN-UPS THINK

Nothing worries pigeons. They know they are safe and sound, well fed and well cared for. This is the opposite of how I feel right now, and explains why I can't seem to say a word.

"What are we going to do?" Viva asks. "Stop breaking world records?"

"I think it was a suggestion," Lonnie says, "not a rule."

"That's true," Viva says. "She never came right out and said we couldn't do it."

"Couldn't do what?" Grumpy Pigeon Man asks, walking into the aviary.

I stand up so he can sit on my bucket. "Aunt Ursula is not a fan of the world records," I say.

"Did she say you have to stop?" he asks.

Lonnie shakes his head. "She suggested we mow the lawn."

He sighs and sits down. "That's the problem with kids these days."

"What is?" Viva asks.

"You care what grown-ups think. In my day, we did just what we wanted. If we wanted to climb a tree, we climbed. If we wanted to dig a hole, we dug it. If we wanted to break a record, we broke it."

"Wait just a second," I say. "Did you try and break records when you were a kid?"

"And what if I did?" he asks. "My point is, breaking a record doesn't hurt anyone, especially not that aunt of yours."

"I don't know," Lonnie says. "Aunt Ursula is pretty scary."

Grumpy Pigeon Man shakes his head. "You know what's scary, getting in the middle of a moose and its dinner. That happened to me when I was hiking in Maine. Luckily, there are lots of trees, which brings me back to if you want to climb a tree, do it, because you never know when learning that skill will come in handy."

"So you ran away from the moose?" Lonnie asks.

"I climbed away," Grumpy Pigeon Man answers. "You'd do the same if you had any brains."

"But what about mowing the lawn?" I ask. "She wants us to mow the lawn."

"You can't mow and break a world record in one day?" Grumpy Pigeon Man stands up. "Youth is wasted on the young." He walks away.

"Sometimes grown-ups are weird," I whisper.

"But at the same time they're so right," Lonnie whispers back.

Viva nods, and then we start planning for the record we'll break.

RULES ABOUT JUMP ROPES

1. Don't believe all those kids on the playground who make it look so easy.
2. Don't skip rope next to anyone because you just end up whacking them with the rope.

3. Don't try breaking a record for fancy tricks with a jump rope, because it's actually more dangerous than you imagine.

MOST EXPENSIVE TOILET

Because it turns out you actually have to know how to skip rope to break a skip-rope record, we move on to mowing the grass. Well, also because Aunt Ursula saw what we were doing and put a stop to it.

"One of my rules is always be prepared," she says.

"That sounds familiar," I say.

"It's a popular rule. In this case, it means be prepared that you will now mow the lawn."

The mower is the kind that is powered by nothing but muscle, and it is almost as impossible to push as the rope was to skip. I'm impressed that Mom and Dad actually mow grass like this. If it was up to me, I'd probably let it grow.

But Aunt Ursula waves from the window, so I keep mowing.

"I think I'll head home," Viva says. "I have my own grass to mow."

Lonnie nods. "If Mom heard I mowed your grass and not ours, she'd never forgive me."

The record for most expensive toilet system in the world is the one used on space ships that cost $23.4 million.

As weird as it is to have to figure out how an astronaut can pee when there is no gravity, the weirder thing is that here I am mowing the lawn.

MOM, HER JOB, AND THE BATS

That night Sharon helps Aunt Ursula cook dinner.

"It's a wonderful skill to have," Aunt Ursula says. "Especially since you're going off to college."

Strange but true, the record for largest bubble-gum bubble blown out of the nose is 11 inches. The woman who broke this record says she started doing it to entertain her children. Tonight Mom comes home from work as if she's broken this record, too. She's so happy and funny and tells us a great story about her day and about saving a guy who was trapped in his bathroom because bats got in his house.

I don't blame him for locking himself in the bathroom. I'd do the same thing if there were seven bats flying around our house, but Mom said that when she found him, he was wearing five hats, a football helmet, a winter coat, mittens, and boots.

We're all laughing and eating Sharon's food, which is surprisingly good considering it's the first meal she's ever cooked. I'm glad Aunt Ursula was the teacher and not Dad. Thinking about the guy in the bathroom makes me think about Sharon in the bathroom and how she hasn't sung since graduation.

Is this what Aunt Ursula meant about having a plan? I look around the table at Grace, Maggie, Caitlin, and Casey. Aunt Ursula couldn't change them. They're like those bats. They'll keep a grown man hiding in his bathroom.

CLEANING THE BASEMENT

As I spread jam on Aunt Ursula's toast this morning she says, "It's clear that you and your friends have been given too much unstructured time. Your parents allowed you to do whatever you want, and what you chose was not that impressive." Aunt Ursula pulls out a piece of paper that must be meant for me. "The mural project doesn't start until Monday, so to help you get through the next few days I've made up a list of things to do. This list will help you focus on things that are more beneficial to others than breaking records."

I hand her the toast and she hands me the list.

The first thing on it is *clean the basement*. There are two reasons why this is not happening.

1. Lonnie and Viva are coming over soon and we need to focus on breaking a record.
2. She hasn't been down in the zombie basement or she would know that there's

as much chance of me cleaning it as there is of me breaking the record for longest motorcycle ride through a tunnel of fire (395 feet 0.15 inches). I'm never doing that.

I keep these reasons to myself because if I told them to her, she'd probably have some rule about why they're ridiculous.

PIGEON POWER

I'm waiting for Lonnie and Viva to show up when I notice Caitlin and Casey. They are at the dining room table surrounded by piles of fabric.

"What's going on?" I ask.

"Aunt Ursula thought we should make uniforms for our business," Caitlin says, looking through the fabric. Most of it has flowers and is bright colored. I don't imagine their uniforms looking like that.

They must agree with me because Casey adds, "She thought we should start with making new curtains for the living room."

"It's easier," they say at the same time, and turn back to their new job.

“Weird,” I say, but everyone is too busy to hear me.

When Lonnie and Viva arrive, we sneak out to the aviary. I pull the list out of my pocket, where I pushed it down, hoping maybe it would be forgotten, or get put through the wash. I hand it to them to read.

1. Clean the basement. (Never.)
2. Mow the lawn. (Again?)
3. Feed Smarty Pants. (I’ll do it, but the smell kills me.)
4. Walk Peanut. (Really?)
5. Vacuum the house. (Could be fun.)
6. Fold laundry. (What’s folding?)

Viva shakes her head. "That is a list of jobs parents are supposed to do."

"What are we going to do?" Lonnie asks.

"If she thinks I'm cleaning the basement," I say, "she really is an optimist."

Lonnie frowns. "I mean about breaking a record. How do we break a record when you have all this to do, and the mural project starts on Monday?"

Viva says, "Grumpy Pigeon Man thinks we can do it."

"Grumpy Pigeon Man doesn't live with Aunt Ursula."

I stare at the pigeons, who do exactly what they always do: sit, coo, and bob their heads. You can always count on pigeons to stay the same.

And that's when I get it. "Pigeon power," I say.

"Pigeon power?" Lonnie asks.

"Pigeons get the job done. They eat, they drink, they bathe, and then they go on with their lives."

"Pigeon power," Viva says. "I like it."

Obi-Wan Kenobi flies over and lands on my shoulder. And for no reason at all, he poos on me.

Getting pooed on at this exact moment proves that I'm absolutely right about pigeon power. We take care of what Aunt Ursula wants us to do, and then we do what we want to do.

It's all about pigeon power.

But first I need to change my clothes.

THE DESTRUCTOR VERSUS JAKE

On my way to put on a clean shirt, I run past The Destructor, who is sitting at the kitchen table, weaving away.

He pulls the stick in and out. He looks so happy, and he's not destroying anything. I should be really happy. Instead, a different kind of thought comes into my head, which is that the new and improved Destructor is actually a little boring.

As soon as I think it, I push it away.

That's the kind of thought that's sillier than the record for eating the most jelly with a chopstick in one minute (1 pound 6 ounces).

I mean, I've dreamed of this day. "Hey, Jake," I say. "Your weaving looks really good."

He smiles a huge smile. It's the first time I've called him Jake for a long time, but it's clear he deserves it.

LONNIE, VIVA, AND ME VERSUS THE LIST

Lonnie, Viva, and I spend the rest of the day going through Aunt Ursula's list.

1. Clean the basement. (Still never.)
2. Mow the lawn. (Lonnie and Viva will not tell their parents.)
3. Feed Smarty Pants. (We plug our noses for this one.)
4. Walk Peanut. (We only walk down the block and back because he barks at us all the way.)
5. Vacuum the house. (It turns out vacuuming up dirt is fun but vacuuming our hair is hilarious.)
6. Fold laundry. (Boring! No wonder Mom and Dad just toss our clothes into our drawers.)

And while we do all those things we think about records we could break.

"Most yardsticks broken over the head in one minute," I suggest.

"Sounds dangerous," Viva says. Viva is probably the bravest person I know, but even she knows when to draw the line.

"Most cartwheels in one minute?" she asks.

"Sounds sickening," I say.

Lonnie offers, "Holding our breath the longest? It's only twenty-two minutes."

We all nod. We stop what we're doing, find a clock, and go! I'm gasping for breath at eighteen seconds, Viva makes it to twenty-three seconds, and Lonnie collapses at thirty-one.

"Not even close," Viva pants as we go back to finding pairs of socks.

The one item from the list that we don't do is clean the basement, but by that time Aunt Ursula is already lying down for her nap, so we figure we can have a little free time.

Sadly, we're all so worn out from chores and imagining records we could break that Lonnie and Viva go home.

Tomorrow is bound to be better.

HOW WRONG CAN I BE?

Since I don't have anything else to do, I decide to head out to the aviary. On my way, I pass Maggie, who I thought was out for a run. She's actually digging up a part of the backyard that just a few hours ago I mowed. "What are you doing?"

"I'm planting a garden." She pushes the shovel in, digs up some grass, and tosses it to the side. "It was Aunt Ursula's idea. She says it will teach me a lot of skills I need for running, like balance, upper-arm strength, and perseverance, but without any injuries, and I'll grow food for the family."

"Weird," I say.

At least there's still Grace. Nothing will change her. Not even Aunt Ursula.

WE DO NOT

The next few days go along the same. Aunt Ursula gives me chores. Things like: water the yard, mop the floors, wash dishes. *Clean the basement* is still there, and will always be there, as far as I'm concerned. Sharon cooks most of the day. Caitlin and Casey hang up the curtain they made, which came out a little crooked, but it was their first try. Now they're working on something else. Maggie digs and waters and weeds her garden. Jake sits there weaving.

Grace still has her camera and doesn't look like she's giving it up for anything. I knew she was strong.

Lonnie, Viva, and I do the chores, and then once Aunt Ursula goes to her room for her nap, we attempt a few world records. Sadly we never get far.

We do not break the record for tallest house of cards (25 feet 9 7/16 inches). We don't come close, not only because it keeps falling down, but also because clearly we need a lot more cards.

We do not break the record for most soap bubbles blown inside one large bubble (152) even though we use up all the dish soap and all of The Destructor's bubble bath trying. Aunt Ursula wakes up during this attempt because we're laughing so hard, but we pretend to be washing the windows.

We also do not break the record for the fastest

mile on a pogo stick (12 minutes 16 seconds) because even though we each have a pogo stick, we're all really bad at it and fall over after three hops.

But none of it matters because Viva grabs the hose and sprays Lonnie and me with water, which leads us to the best water fight ever. And we wouldn't have done that if we'd broken a record.

MOM, HER JOB, AND EMUS

Tonight, Mom and I are sitting together, just the two of us, in the living room. Mom is telling me about capturing an escaped emu.

"An emu?" I ask.

"It's like an ostrich."

"Ostriches hold the world record for fastest birds on land."

Mom smiles. "I did not know that."

I nod. "So the emu escaped from its home?" I ask.

"Yes, someone in the next town over keeps them as pets."

"Do a lot of people keep emus as pets?"

"Not in our town. There are a lot of rules about what kinds of birds you can keep and how many. For instance, you're allowed three chickens, but no more, and no roosters at all."

"Going back to the emu, how did you catch it?"

"Very, very carefully. They are fast, so I couldn't outrun it. I had to use my brains." She taps the side of her head with her finger. "I know that emus like berries, so I went to the store and bought bags and bags of berries, and the emu couldn't resist me."

I smile and think about how amazing Mom is

to have this job, and to help people and animals, and to be so good at it.

If Lonnie were here, he would probably know some great Star Wars quote to sum up this situation, but he's not, and the only quote I can think of is C-3PO saying "We're doomed" and doesn't apply to my family right now.

No, right now everything is going great.

LARGEST METAL COIL

Lonnie and Viva have been dragged off for the weekend with their families. They'll be back for the mural project on Monday.

Today, I cleaned the upstairs bathroom, and since Sharon isn't hogging it anymore, I had all the time I needed to clean it properly.

"It's wonderful," Aunt Ursula gushed. "It's perfect for my spa treatment." And then she went in with Peanut and locked the door.

Now, I'm having quiet time on the sofa and looking through the world record book that Ms. Raffeli gave me. It's got a lot more words and a lot less pictures, so you really have to concentrate.

Grace plops down next to me. I protect my face before she can shove her camera into it and protect my feet before she slams down on them. But she doesn't do either. Instead, she pulls out a pad of paper and starts writing on it.

"What are you doing?" Grace has never been one to keep her thoughts to herself.

"What does it look like? I'm writing."

"You hate to write. That's why you take photographs."

"Aunt Ursula has a rule about photographs."

"What rule?" I ask.

"That it's rude to hold up a camera and click it in someone's face."

I suddenly realize Aunt Ursula is even stronger than Grace.

Strange but true, the record for longest metal

coil passed through the nose and out the mouth is 11 feet 10.91 inches. It doesn't seem possible, but it is and no brain is injured. Except mine, which hurts just thinking about it. This is the same as how I feel about Grace giving up photography. It hurts my brain.

"Don't you miss photography?" I ask.

"It's only been an hour. Anyway, Aunt Ursula says it would help Mom." Grace looks around, checking to see if anyone is close to us. She whispers, "The truth is, I'd do a lot more than this if it helped Mom."

And I'm left wondering what our family will be like now that my siblings have all changed. I know I should be happy, because it's what I've always said I wanted. But it turns out getting what you've always wanted isn't quite as satisfying as I thought.

CHORES. LOTS OF CHORES.

I finished my chores for today, which included dusting the bookshelves, so I am now hanging out with the pigeons, watching them fluff themselves, and missing Lonnie and Viva, when Grumpy Pigeon Man comes out.

"You're looking nice today," I say, which is true.

He's wearing what Dad calls trousers, instead of his normal blue jeans, and spiffy red suspenders hold them up. His shirt looks like it's been ironed, and if I didn't know better I'd say his boots have been polished.

"These old things." He frowns. He sits down next to me. "Your house seems pretty quiet these days. What's going on?"

I shrug.

"If there's one thing I don't trust it's a quiet kid. It always means they're up to no good."

I shake my head. "Aunt Ursula has everyone busy. Sharon's cooking, the twins are sewing, Maggie's growing a vegetable patch, Grace is writing, and The Destructor is weaving."

"What are you doing?"

"Chores," I say. "Lots of chores."

THE NEAREST STAR TO THE SUN

At that moment, the back door opens and Peanut charges. He runs straight to the fence, barking madly.

Aunt Ursula follows. Her hair is done up fancy, and I can see she's wearing lipstick. She calls and calls for Peanut to come. He doesn't, but when the pigeons flock to the side closest to Peanut and coo at him he stops barking.

"Get that dog away," growls Grumpy Pigeon Man. "He's scaring my pigeons!" It seems pretty clear that they have decided not to be scared of this dog anymore. I do not point this out. I don't think he would appreciate it.

"If you didn't keep those pigeons Peanut wouldn't have to protect me."

"My pigeons are not a problem."

"Your pigeons have always been a problem. Maybe no one said it, but it's true."

"I choose to disagree, Ursula."

"Those pigeons should not be here, and you know it," Aunt Ursula says.

I'm sure she doesn't mean that, but it's very upsetting to hear. It's one thing to change everyone in my family. It's another to change the pigeons.

But Grumpy Pigeon Man and Aunt Ursula keep yelling at each other.

I trudge home because listening to them fight is like traveling 18,000 years to reach the nearest star to the sun. I don't care if I'd get to ride in a rocket ship. Traveling for that long would not be fun.

SOMETHING'S WRONG

Mom has been on the phone for a while. I'm pretty sure she's talking to her boss, but it's weird because it's a Sunday, and why would they talk on the weekend? But Mom steers clear of us until she hangs up and collapses on the sofa.

Sharon offers her a snack, something called a macaron, which is like an Oreo but fancier. I stole one when she wasn't looking, and I wasn't that impressed. I'd take a good old Oreo any day.

She notices right away how much I dusted today. "This room has never been cleaner."

Caitlin and Casey walk in. They are wearing matching shirts that they sewed with huge embroidered cursive *C*s on the back.

Aunt Ursula looks at Caitlin. "Well done, Casey! Those buttons were hard." Then she looks at Casey and says, "Caitlin, I didn't think you'd get the collar right, but you did."

Mom doesn't correct her. And neither do the rest of us.

Maggie shows Mom the carrot seeds she's about to plant.

"They're so tiny," Mom says.

Grace hands Mom a pile of papers and smiles. "They're the first pages of the novel I'm writing."

"You've gotten so far," Mom says.

Jake bustles in and presses something into her hand. "This is for you."

"Oh." Mom holds it up. "What is it?"

"Woven underpants."

Mom's eyes get big. "Just what I've always wanted."

And the great thing about Mom is when she says this, she really means it. The other great thing about Mom is that she can make the weirdest thing in the world, like woven underwear, feel so normal.

For all Mom's sweetness and smiles she's totally reminding me of the cusk eel. The cusk eel is the record holder for the fish that lives the deepest under water (27,460 feet below the surface). That's deep. There's something about the way Mom is acting that makes me feel like she's hiding something from us about as deep down as the cusk eel.

WEIRDER

At dinner when I ask what's wrong, she says, "My job is not always easy."

"I knew something was wrong," I say.

"I can't talk about it. But I'm working very hard to solve it." And then she bursts into tears and hugs me.

This is definitely weirder than the time Mom decided we needed to play more family games, like Monopoly. That lasted a day and ended in a fight so huge that she put all the games in the basement until "we were old enough to handle them."

The games have never been brought back out.

I wonder if Mom can handle her problem the same way.

For some reason, I doubt it.

JULY

MURAL PROJECT BEGINS

The mural project is right next door to where Mom works, so she brings Jake and me. It's really odd being out in public with Jake because he's so different than he ever was before.

First off, he's wearing a T-shirt and shorts and not cans or pigeon feathers as he has been doing for months. He's also not telling everyone to call him Can Boy or Pigeon Boy. Besides that, he's careful with how he uses his body—he doesn't crash into anyone. He's not digging through trash, scraping up pigeon poo, or causing random destruction.

I mean, really, he's a different kid.

"This is where everyone is meeting," Mom says as she parks the car. "There's Viva's mom. You go on over; Ms. Cecile will be there."

I don't see Ms. Cecile, but I do see Lonnie and Viva, and a few other kids I know, like Lewis, Ny, Angus, and the two Jasmines. There's also a bunch of other kids I don't know of all ages, from the kindergarten buddies to some kids who look like teenagers.

Seeing all those kids makes me feel nervous. There are already so many, but Jake looks even more scared, so I grab our lunches and take Jake by the hand, and we climb out of the car together.

Mom follows. "I know it's a lot to ask, but try not to visit me at work." She hugs Jake. "Aunt Ursula will pick you up. Oh, and don't forget to have fun." She gives us one last hug and runs off to her office.

Jake and I run to Lonnie and Viva. Together again! We high-five each other, which is as unsuccessful as ever.

Jake looks around. "Who's the teacher?"

Lonnie says, "She's not here."

"No one knows why." Viva shrugs. Viva's mom stands off to the side talking on her phone. A couple of other parents stand close to her. I don't know who she is calling, but if anyone can sort this out, Viva's mom will. I don't know what her job is, but it definitely has something to do with sorting out problems.

Ny, Cornelio, the two Jasmines, Lewis, and Serena all rush over. Then they see Jake and they circle around him, asking loads of questions, like, "Where are the cans?" and "What should we call you?"

"Jake," he answers, which is so normal, it's boring.

When Viva's mom finally comes over she doesn't look happy. "I can't find anyone who knows what is going on."

Jake frowns and grabs my hand tighter. And even though at first I didn't want to do this project, the thought of it being canceled is not at all appealing. I'm tired of chores.

Suddenly, there's a honk behind us. We all look for Ms. Cecile, but it isn't Ms. Cecile climbing out of the car. It's someone way better. It's Ms. Raffeli! And she's wearing jean shorts and a T-shirt that says, "If you can read this, thank a teacher. If you can't, go back to school!" She never wore clothes like that to school.

Seeing Ms. Raffeli is like breaking the world

record for being hit by a car eight times in two minutes and coming out of it without a Band-Aid.

The relief is tremendous.

TOGETHER AGAIN

"Ms. Raffeli!" Viva runs over and gives her a big hug, and then the two Jasmines and Ny run over and I hug her, too. And then Jake squeezes in and hugs Ms. Raffeli.

"Are you going to be our teacher?" Lonnie asks.

"Your Jedi skills are, as always, excellent, Lonnie. And let me state for the record that this is not how I pictured my summer." She pauses, looks around at all of us, and says, "But it could be worse." A tiny smile creeps up the corner of her mouth as she opens the back of her car, which is full of notepads, pencils, paints, and brushes.

"Do you have experience with painting a mural?" Viva's mom asks.

"Nope, none at all."

Viva's mom looks a little rattled by this answer, but that's Ms. Raffeli for you; she's always honest.

"I'm sure we'll figure it out."

You can tell Viva's mom isn't sure about leaving, but she doesn't have much choice; she's got a job to go to. So she kisses Viva good-bye. "Call me if you need anything."

Viva shakes her head. "My mom is so embarrassing."

"I like how she pays attention," I say.

"She's a lot like Aunt Ursula." Jake smiles.

"She's got just about as many rules," Viva agrees. "But she doesn't make cupcakes."

"Come on." Ms. Raffeli scoots us to her car. "Lots to do and we're already late."

As we carry stuff out and over to the picnic table, Ms. Raffeli explains that Ms. Cecile just got a job in Puerto Toro, Chile.

"Did you know that Puerto Toro, Chile, is the southernmost permanently inhabited place in the world? I know this because it is a record."

Ms. Raffeli hands me a box of brushes and says, "It's day one of the mural project, could we please save world records until day four?"

TOGETHER AGAIN PART 2

After everything is unpacked Ms. Raffeli waves her hand to show us the outside wall we'll be painting. It's on one side of City Hall, next to a park and a parking lot. The parking lot isn't very interesting, but the park has a couple of nice trees that make me think about Grumpy Pigeon Man's advice about climbing a tree.

As if Ms. Raffeli can read my mind, she says, "There will be no climbing of those trees. I don't want a broken arm while you're with me."

Then she leads us into City Hall. I see a sign that points to Mom's office, but I don't say anything to Jake because I'm not sure what he'll do, and Mom asked us not to bother her.

Ms. Raffeli has us sit in the main entry on marble stairs that lead up to the second floor. It's an old building with tall windows and a huge door. "We'll decide on the theme for the mural later, although it will definitely have something to do with our city. But first we will draw."

Viva raises her hand. "I wish you had done a mystery bag."

Lewis says, "I was going to say that."

Ny covers her face in her hands.

Lonnie says, "Mystery bag was genius, but Ms. Raffeli probably didn't have time."

Jasmine B. smiles. "I think this is great."

"Me too," Jasmine H. says. "And anyway, Lewis was the only one who guessed them."

In school, this would be about the time Ms. Raffeli's eyebrows would rise up her forehead, but here she shrugs and says, "Sadly, as much as I also like mystery bag, Lonnie is correct. I wasn't given enough notice. But now to the work ahead. We will begin by meeting outside every morning."

Angus hops over. "What if it's raining?"

"Then we'll meet here. We don't have a lot of time to make a mural, so we must stay focused."

Lonnie raises his hand. "I just want to say I've got a good feeling about this."

"I'm glad one of us does, Lonnie," Ms. Raffeli says. "But no matter what happens, I'm sure it's going to be interesting."

Jake looks at Ms. Raffeli like she's the most powerful Jedi of them all and says, "Ms. Raffeli, if Princess Leia survived all those awesome adventures, you can survive this. I know you can."

LONGEST TIME

We spread out in small groups with our pads and paper. My group is Lonnie, Viva, and of course Jake. We draw anything we want that we can see with our eyes.

I'm drawing a trash can. Lonnie draws a door. Viva draws a bench. Jake draws a window and what he sees out the window, like a pigeon, which I wish I had picked to draw because drawing a trash can is boring. It's also really hard to sit still. All I want to do is get up, move around, draw something else, or talk to Lonnie or Viva.

But every time I feel like that, Ms. Raffeli happens to circle past. She says, "Good." Or, "Nice shading." Or, "Don't give up."

At one point she says, "If you're done with your picture, turn the paper over and draw the

same thing again, from a different angle."

"Aggghh!" I moan.

"You can do it. Notice what's the same? What changes?"

The weird thing is that the longer I sit and draw, the longer I feel like I can sit and draw, like my brain doesn't squirm so much. And the coolest thing is that the longer I sit and draw, the more things about the trash can I see, like how there are scratches on one side, and a dent at the top.

I can tell this isn't just me. Jake is doing it.

When Ms. Raffeli finally says, "Stop," I'm amazed that I sat so long. Honestly, it feels like I broke a record.

IT'S SO NORMAL, IT'S WEIRD

After muraling, Aunt Ursula picks up Lonnie, Viva, Jake, and me. As soon as we arrive home, my stomach tightens. I don't know why, since there's a yummy smell of cake and nothing else out of control going on in our house.

I mean, stuff is going on, but it's not dangerous, loud, or out of place.

Sharon sits in the kitchen with a cookbook in her face. I hear the sewing machine whirring away upstairs. Maggie walks in and washes her dirt-covered hands. Then I hear an odd tapping sound from Grace's room.

Aunt Ursula says, "I found an old typewriter for Grace. She seems to like it more than a computer or paper and pen." She cuts us slices of the cake.

Jake plunks down in front of his weaving.

Lonnie looks at me. "There's really something different about your family now that Aunt Ursula has moved in."

"It's true." Viva nods, taking a bite of cake. "But I can't put my finger on it."

Lonnie takes one too, then says, "It's so normal, it's weird."

I nod because really, I couldn't have said it better myself.

IT'S SO NORMAL, IT'S WEIRD PART 2

Aunt Ursula sends us to the backyard to rake up stray leaves from last fall. Dad is a big raker, mostly because Grumpy Pigeon Man yells at him about it, but even so, there is a surprisingly large amount of leaves that got left behind.

We sneak out a copy of *The Guinness Book of World Records* with us. Every time we walk past it, we turn a page and read. That's how we find the "most pull-ups in one minute" record (43).

And after we finish the raking we try. I haven't hung off the monkey bars on our old play set in a long time. Last time I had to jump for them, and this time my knees practically touch the ground. But that's not why we can't beat it. We can't beat it because after twelve pull-ups my arms turn to noodles, and the same is true for Lonnie and Viva.

"How about something using chopsticks?" Viva suggests.

"As long as it doesn't use any muscles," I say, "I'll do it."

So we sneak into the house and grab some. As it turns out we don't need to sneak, because Aunt Ursula is napping, and my sisters are busy. Not even Jake asks what we're doing. There used to be a time when we couldn't get rid of him! Now he doesn't even care.

I look at his weaving. "Can I try?" I ask.

Lonnie and Viva look at me like I'm crazy. I admit, even I'm surprised.

But he nods and shows me what to do. "No," he corrects. "Under, then over." I try again. "Stop, Teddy. You're destroying it." He pushes me out of the way and sighs very loudly.

STORM CLOUDS APPROACHING

"Is this a real record?" I ask. We're all lying on the grass with our chopsticks, trying to pick as many blades of grass in one minute as we can.

"I don't think so," Viva says. "I just thought it would be cool."

I have to say, she's right.

Lonnie says, "I'm up to nine blades, how about you?"

"I'm up to twelve." Viva smiles.

I ask, "Did anyone set the timer?"

"We're practicing and then I'll turn it on," Viva says.

"If we get really good at chopsticks we should try to break a whole bunch of records with them," Lonnie says.

I nod happily.

Out of nowhere Aunt Ursula's foot appears right in the middle of the patch of grass we're all trying to pick from. "What's going on here?"

We stop and look up. She's looking down.

Strange but true, the longest uninterrupted live TV weather report lasted 34 hours. There must have been lots of different weather conditions moving through during that time. Aunt Ursula only looks like the storm clouds.

BAD WEATHER HITS

"I thought I made my feelings understood," Aunt Ursula says.

Viva says, "Technically, we are mowing the lawn."

Lonnie and I nod in agreement. I am impressed by Viva's quick thinking.

"I understand that in the past you have not been asked to uphold rules of childhood behavior, but that is what I am asking of you. To be clear, breaking world records is not one of the rules."

Before Aunt Ursula says any more, the back door opens and Jake yells, "Peanut wants you."

Peanut springs out the door and sprints right past Aunt Ursula, running straight for the fence closest to the pigeons, where he lies down, and rolls over on his back. The pigeons coo at him.

As weird as this is, I can't think about it because all I know is that Lonnie, Viva, and I are not supposed to try to break a world record ever again.

RULES ABOUT PIGEONS

After Aunt Ursula lays down the law about world records, Lonnie, Viva, and I are not in the mood for much. So they head home and I head for the aviary.

If the pigeons were to write down a list of rules for themselves I think this is what it would say:

1. Always flutter around Teddy when he walks in.
2. Always crowd around when Teddy serves food.
3. Always take a moment to sit on Teddy's knee, shoulder, or top of head.
4. If the opportunity arises, always poo on Teddy. He clearly loves it.

MILK-SHAKE HAPPINESS

I come straight in and take a shower. When I'm done Aunt Ursula asks if I will take out the recycling. I do. She doesn't say a single thing more about Lonnie, Viva, and me breaking world records. I plan to talk to Mom and Dad about it, but when they get home, they look stressed out, and keep having whispered conversations by the sink, where all I can hear is Mom saying, "I'm trying everything I can, but it's a law."

And Dad whispering, "I'm sure there's some way around it."

Aunt Ursula is as nice to me as always for the

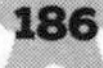

rest of the night, and in the morning when Mom, Jake, and I leave, she makes a special effort to tell me to have a good day.

Now that world records are off-limits, the mural is all I have.

Today Ms. Raffeli has us draw some buildings in our sketchbooks. We're sitting in front of the town hall looking out at the street. Tall brick and concrete buildings surround us.

"Notice the space in between the buildings as much as the buildings themselves," she says.

"How do I draw space?" I ask.

Viva says, "Start with your foot, and draw everything that is around your foot, or everything that is not your foot."

"That makes my head hurt," I say.

Lonnie puts down his pencil. "Like Yoda says, 'you must unlearn what you have learned.'"

"You are not helping." I hit him on the head with my pencil.

Lonnie holds up his hand, spreading his fingers out. "Can you see the V?"

I nod.

"That's what you want to draw."

I decide to draw a tree, or should I say, everything that is not the tree. It turns out that everything that is not the tree are shapes, like triangles and rectangles and shapes with no names.

And when I finally finish, I hold up my picture to show Lonnie and Viva, and that's when Jake grabs the picture out of my hand.

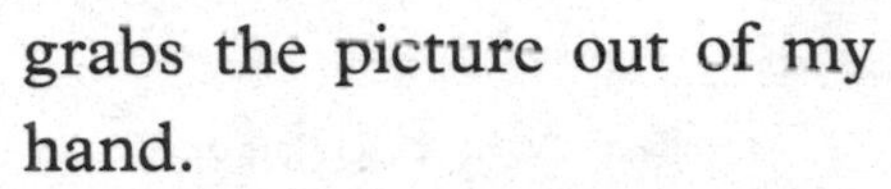

"Hey, give it back!" He's spent so many years destroying my things; it's impossible to trust him.

But all he does is run over to Ms. Raffeli and show her.

"That is good," she says.

Lonnie and Viva agree.

I'm pretty sure I haven't felt this happy since I read about Gary Bashaw Jr., who broke the record for most milk shake dispensed through his nose, which means he made a milk shake in his mouth, shot it out of his nose, and got it to land into a glass.

That record always makes me happy.

JULY FOURTH

July Fourth is a holiday, so there's no work for Mom or Dad, and no mural class. Instead our whole family gets ready for the annual city picnic and fireworks show.

Sharon and Aunt Ursula have been cooking all day. Caitlin and Casey sewed red, white, and blue napkins and a tablecloth. Maggie brings in lettuce from her garden, her first crop. Grace has written a poem, which she will recite at our picnic. And Jake wove straw plates for everyone to use.

I don't have anything to share but have done a terrific job cleaning up after everyone!

We all pile into the van and head to the city park. It's already teeming with people. Aunt Ursula asks me to carry a lot of the stuff because her arms are full with Peanut. We're meeting Lonnie and his family, and Viva and her family. We spot them right away because Viva's dad is holding up a flag with their family name on it. I laugh. My family would never have a flag.

Viva shrugs. "Dad wanted to be sure I could always find them if I ever get lost."

"Makes sense," Lonnie says.

Viva shakes her head. "It made sense when I was five; now it's just embarrassing."

Peanut starts barking madly because Grumpy Pigeon Man arrives. Peanut squirms out of Aunt Ursula's arms, runs to him, and rolls over.

"Peanut," Aunt Ursula says. "Mummy is here."

But Peanut keeps licking Grumpy Pigeon Man. It's clear to all of us that Peanut has decided he likes Grumpy Pigeon Man, but none of us say a word.

I make room for him on our blanket. "I didn't know you were coming."

"Your mother called. Said I should." He jerks his head to Aunt Ursula and whispers, "Didn't know she'd be here, though."

I can tell he's thinking about leaving, but Mom dumps a pile of food on his plate and says, "Have you thought about what I said?"

Grumpy Pigeon Man shakes his head.

I wonder what they would need to talk about. But I don't think about it for long because Lonnie and Viva jump up with a beach ball and the three of us bat it around. Not to break a record but for fun.

Finally, the fireworks begin. It's a crazy combination of exciting, beautiful, and extremely loud.

When they're done Grace stands up to read her poem. "If we know ourselves—" But she doesn't get any further because Peanut cuts her off.

"Rrar! Rrar-rrar-rar."

Grace crosses her arms and says, "Everyone's a critic." And cracks up at her own joke. We all laugh, too, because what else can we do?

BECAUSE

Because Ms. Raffeli said we should all start brainstorming images for the mural, Lonnie and Viva go straight home to work on ideas.

Because I don't feel inspired to draw, I wander into the kitchen, where Sharon and Jerome are cooking together. Sharon is beating something in a bowl. Jerome is singing some song I don't know about sitting on a dock of a bay and watching the tide roll away.

"Can I help?" I ask Sharon.

"Baked Alaska takes a lot of muscle." I don't know what baked Alaska is but it's clear that besides muscle, it takes a lot of eggs.

"Singing takes muscles, too," Jerome says. It's also clear that Jerome really misses singing with Sharon. Jerome takes the whisk out of her hands and starts beating the eggs.

Because Sharon won't let me help I drift into the living room, where Caitlin and Casey have patterns spread out all over the floor. Caitlin looks up at Casey, and Casey passes her a pincushion full of pins. A second later, Casey looks up at Caitlin and Caitlin passes her the scissors.

Because I can't help them, I go looking for Maggie, who's outside dumping old food scraps into a barrel.

"Is that compost?" I ask.

She nods and stirs it.

"Compost like Jake wanted to make."

She nods again. "It's great for the garden."

Just because compost is great for a garden doesn't mean it's interesting.

Because Grace is sitting in the old play set typing away, I stand over her shoulder and try to read what she's writing.

She doesn't even look up or do anything, not even stomp on my foot.

That's why I go up to my room. Jake is there. He's set up his loom on my desk.

I plop down next him.

"Can I try weaving again?" I touch the strings

but he pushes my hand away.

"Please," I say. I reach over and grab the stick that he's weaving with. "I won't mess it up this time. I promise." I start to bring it through. "In and out," I say. "See, I got it."

But Jake grabs it out of my hand. "Teddy! You messed it up again."

He undoes what I just did.

"You want to come out to the aviary?"

"No thanks," he says.

"How about the trash?" I ask, even though I am shocked that I am asking for his company. "Do we need to go through it?"

"No," he says. "I've got work to do."

I'm struck by how all my siblings are acting just like I've always wanted. But like the world record for the first person to vomit in space, nothing prepares you for it.

RULES ABOUT CHORES

1. Doing the same thing every day is boring. Unless it's breaking a world record, feeding the pigeons, or drawing pictures. (So maybe it's chores that are the problem.)

NAMING PIGEONS

Ms. Raffeli walks us over to the public library so we can research possible local history topics for the mural. Viva closes her books. "It's all so depressing."

Lonnie says, "I like history."

Jake holds up a magazine. "Look!" He pushes it right into Lonnie's face.

Lonnie takes it from Jake. "Whoa! Teddy, Viva, check this out." The magazine is all about Star Wars and a new movie!

Now that is big news.

Lonnie reads. "It's all very secretive, but old characters will be back, and new ones will be introduced." We squeeze in closer to him, crowding around to see it better.

Lonnie flips through the magazine. Viva stops him. "Pictures."

"New characters." Lonnie gets a huge smile on his face. For Jake's sake, he shows each character and says their name. "Rey, Finn—"

"Who's that?" Jake asks, pointing to an orange-and-white-looking ball.

Viva reads. "A new droid—BB-8!"

"This is going to be great," Lonnie says. "I can tell."

"You know what this means?" I ask. Lonnie, Viva, and Jake shake their heads. "We can name more pigeons!"

THE DARK SIDE

Viva takes out her pad of paper and draws jet fighters. "We should do something about Star Wars."

"How do jet fighters have anything to do with our city?" I ask.

"Star Wars has to do with everything."

Lonnie opens his pad and shows me a picture of a bunch of dogs. "Did you know that our city was the first city in our state to have an animal shelter?"

"I didn't know that," I say.

Jake leans in. "I really like Peanut."

"How about you, Teddy?" Viva asks. "Any ideas?"

I shake my head.

"What?" Lonnie pulls out my pad. "You must have something." But when he flips through it he sees I don't.

"Careful of the Dark Side," Lonnie warns.

"How is not having an idea going to lead me to the Dark Side?"

"I don't know, but I'm pretty sure it happens,"

Lonnie explains. "So come on, let's get drawing!"

He hands me a pencil and starts sketching out a mural of our city. I add pigeons, he adds some dogs, Jake adds some strange brightly colored lines that look a lot like a rainbow but not curved, and Viva reaches in to draw Chewbacca walking through it.

"Now this," I say, "is a good idea. It has nothing to do with local history, but it's still a really good idea."

RULES ABOUT SUGGESTING A MURAL

1. Surprise people by suggesting something no one thought you would, like Viva, who thought of an airplane theme based on

the history of our local airport. (Instead of Star Wars.)

2. Suggest a piece of local history, like Lonnie, who imagined a whole mural dedicated to women who have changed our city. (Instead of the first animal shelter.)
3. Offer something brightly colored, like Jake, who proposes a mural of multicolored stripes. (Instead of anything to do with anything.)
4. Brainstorm more ideas, because Aunt Ursula says there are rules about what can go on a city mural and she's pretty sure "world records broken by ten-year-olds" falls on the side of *no.* (Even if it is local history.)

MS. RAFFELI'S RULES

The next day it's raining, so we're all inside. Ms. Raffeli announces the theme for the mural. "This was not an easy decision. There were so many ideas, and I'm sure we'll be able to work a lot of them into the final mural. But I finally chose Ny's." Everyone claps, probably because Ny is so nice that it's easy to be happy for her. Ms. Raffeli

turns to Ny. "Would you like to tell everyone about it?"

Ny smiles. "My idea is about jobs that people do in our city."

Without being asked we all start shouting out jobs. Waitress, sales clerk, artist, teacher, bus driver, police officer, mayor; the list goes on and on, and honestly I think we could go on for a lot longer, but Ms. Raffeli stops us. "For the next hour, we will break into small groups and sketch people in City Hall doing their jobs. I've prepared the adults about this."

Then she explains that the rules are:

1. We have to stay in groups no bigger than three. (Buddies not included.)
2. We can't disrupt any work going on.
3. We must be drawing.
4. Please don't let her down or the mayor will never forgive her.

I hope she's joking about this last rule. The mayor really should *not* blame her for anything we do!

THE PIGEON SITUATION

Lewis and Ny and Serena and their buddies go to the mayor's office, some other kids go into the city planner's office, Angus and the two Jasmines head off to the retirement offices, and some other kids go into the parking ticket office.

Lonnie, Viva, Jake, and I go to Mom's office. The office is basically one big room, and in the middle is a counter and Mom and her boss sit on the other side of the counter, except he's not here right now.

"Hey, Mom," Jake says as we walk in. Mom waves, but stays at her desk.

"Jake," I say, "remember Ms. Raffeli's rule. No bothering them." I hand him his pad of paper and pencil. Mom smiles.

Mom is doing a really bad job pretending we're not here. For instance, she picks up her phone and makes a funny face into it.

We all have to muffle our giggles.

Mom stops when her boss walks in, and we draw them sitting at their desks, which is good for drawing but not very interesting.

Lonnie leans over. "Let's go somewhere else," he whispers.

Viva nods.

Just as we're standing up, Mom's boss turns to

her. “Have you handled that pigeon situation yet?”

She freezes, looks at me, and then clears her throat. “I’m investigating it.”

“Well, speed it up. We don’t want—”

“Ahhh-chooo!” Mom sneezes, then sneezes a bunch more. “Ah-choo! Ah-choo! Ah-choo!” I’ve never seen her sneeze so much. By the time she’s done sneezing her boss is on the phone.

“Come on,” Viva nudges. “Let’s go down to the basement and look for the janitor.”

“Do you think there are zombies down there?” Jake asks.

“Hopefully,” Viva says, and leads us out the door.

I stop at the door. Mom smiles at me and I smile back. I hope the pigeon situation is nothing, but for some reason it gives me more shivers than Viva talking about zombies.

SAME AND DIFFERENT

Two weeks go by and not much has changed. It’s still July and it’s still hot. My family is still weird in a normal way. Mom still has her job, I still do chores, and Lonnie, Viva, and I are still not allowed to try and break records.

So it's really exciting when Ms. Raffeli finally says, "Today, we will start painting."

We all let out a cheer!

Ms. Raffeli took our drawings and combined them. "I've drawn out a plan." She shows us the small version. "It's like a map of where we will paint on the walls. First we'll need to draw the map, and then we start putting in colors."

"Like color by number?" Jake asks.

"Exactly," Ms. Raffeli says.

She gives each small group a section to paint. Jake and I paint side by side. He doesn't drip or even get paint on me.

Painting is good for thinking, so as I paint I think about Jake and how he used to make me feel like I was swallowing eighteen swords while juggling three objects at the same time. And now, even though he is well behaved I still feel like I'm swallowing swords and juggling.

It's weird how different someone can be but still feel the same.

DANGER

That afternoon, I go out to feed the birds. I'm on 599 when Grumpy Pigeon Man charges in. The pigeons fly up as he waves a piece of paper in the air. "Do you know about this?"

"About what?"

Grumpy Pigeon Man paces back and forth. "That aunt of yours. She's crossed the line this time."

"Crossed which line?"

"She won't get away with this."

"Won't get away with what?" I wish he'd just answer one of my questions.

"If she thinks she can get rid of my pigeons and that dog can stay, she's got another think coming."

"Get rid of what pigeons?" I ask. My heart

starts beating faster than the clogs worn by Andre Ortolf when he broke the record for running the fastest 100 meters in clogs (16.27 seconds).

"My pigeons. These pigeons. Our pigeons." He gasps. "It's all here. In this letter."

I grab the letter. It's written on fancy stationery from the animal control officer with Mom's name on the bottom. I don't understand anything it says except "not legal to have pigeons within the city limits."

My brain races. The law about birds. Mom being so upset. Mom's boss talking about a pigeon situation. It was these pigeons. But Mom would never tell on Grumpy Pigeon Man.

"It's Ursula's fault." He paces back and forth; the pigeons fly up all around, and then land on him like they know that something is terribly wrong. "It has to be Ursula's fault."

DANGER PART 2

Peanut tears out of the house, running straight for the aviary, barking all the way. When he gets to the fence, he screeches to a stop and sits. His tail wags back and forth.

Aunt Ursula follows him into the yard, looking as fancy as the lettering on that horrible letter. "Peanut," she calls. "Come back this instant."

The pigeons gather closer to Peanut, cooing madly at him, only the wire mesh separating them.

"How could you?" Grumpy Pigeon Man grumps at Aunt Ursula. "It's one thing to fight with me, but this is going too far."

Aunt Ursula looks confused. "I don't know what you're talking about."

"Ohhh," Grumpy Pigeon Man growls, "don't pretend you aren't the one who told them about me."

"Told who about what?"

"My pigeons! You told animal control about my pigeons, and now they're going to take them away from me."

Aunt Ursula's face turns beet red and she walks closer to the aviary. "I have no idea what you're talking about, but I don't like your tone of voice. I had nothing to do with this."

Peanut raises a paw and whimpers at the fence.

He pokes his nose through, trying to find a way to the other side. "You only have yourself to blame. You knew it was against the rules to keep them as pets."

"You planned this all along!"

"I have nothing to say." She scoops Peanut up. As she strides away, Peanut turns back to the pigeons and whines.

"I know that woman is to blame," Grumpy Pigeon Man says. "She's the only one who hates the pigeons."

I try to move, but my legs are stuck as my brain wraps around what's going on. I still don't understand exactly what's happening. "They're going to take the pigeons away?"

Grumpy Pigeon Man crumples up on a bucket.

"When?" I ask. My eyes have started burning.

"Tomorrow," he says.

Tomorrow is the worst thing in the world.

YELLING DOESN'T COUNT

I crash into the house. I stomp into the kitchen. I kick the wall because I can't think of anything else to do. Aunt Ursula marches into the kitchen and I stop attacking the wall.

It's clear she's still upset, but not in a sad way, not like she actually feels sorry for Grumpy Pigeon Man and his pigeons, but upset in a way like he's the one who did something wrong. "They should have taken those pigeons away years ago. And he knows it."

The fastest time to burst 200 balloons with a nail is 33.74 seconds. At this exact second, I feel like I'm all those balloons being burst with a nail. "How could you do this?" I yell. I've never yelled at a grown-up who isn't Mom or Dad before, but I can't stop myself. And just because I don't know what else to do I kick the refrigerator.

"Teddy," she says. "I will talk about this, but not if you yell or kick. That's the rule."

I nod because if I open my mouth I'll either yell or kick.

Aunt Ursula sits down. She points to a seat, but my body won't let me sit. "There is a law in this city that pigeons cannot be kept as pets."

"What kind of crazy law is that?" I blurt out.

She stops and looks at me.

I collapse onto a chair because suddenly I'm so tired I can't stand up anymore.

"The law was put into place years ago. I don't know the history, but it's there, and Tom—I mean, Grumpy Pigeon Man, has been breaking it all these years."

I feel like I can't breathe. Not even Darth Vader breathing. "How do you know that?"

"I was a judge. I retired this year." That explains all her rules and why she came now. "Someone must have finally told the animal control offices about his pigeons. Your mother had no choice. It's the law."

My eyes get blurry. "Did you do it?"

She shakes her head.

"You hate his pigeons. You knew about the law." I wipe my eyes.

"That's true, and I did think about reporting him, but I didn't."

"You fight with him all the time." A tear trickles down my face.

"It doesn't mean I would tell on him." Aunt Ursula takes my hands.

I pull away and stand up. "The pigeons weren't hurting anyone!" I yell, and I know I'm breaking a rule, but I don't care.

"The rules of the law are strong. It's not fair if one person follows them and another one doesn't."

And because she cares more about rules than anything else, and because I feel like I just broke the record for eating 99 fire torches in one minute, I don't say another word, but run straight upstairs.

RULES FOR TRUSTING GROWN-UPS

1. Don't do it. Ever.

STOMPING MAD

I'm so mad I stomp into the bathroom, slam the door, and take a shower. I let the water pound on my head. I'm so mad at myself for going along with Aunt Ursula's rules. For thinking that they made our lives better, for stopping breaking records, and doing chores when all the time she was just keeping me busy so she could get rid of the pigeons.

And then I remember Mom's signature on the bottom of the letter. My throat burns. How could she do that?

I'm never talking to her again. Maybe I'll never leave this shower. They can feed me here, and I'll sleep in the tub, because if the pigeons are gone, then what's the point?

But after ten minutes of the water beating on my brain I start to feel different. My brain begins to click away. I'm not giving up. Those pigeons need me. I'm a world record breaker. Nothing can stop me. I climb out of the shower with one thing on my mind: saving the pigeons.

RULES ABOUT SAVING PIGEONS

1. Save them all.
2. Save them secretly.
3. Save them forever.

THINK FAST

As soon as I'm all dry, and in clean clothes, I call Lonnie from my parents' bedroom and tell him all about the pigeons.

"What can I do?" he asks.

"Call Viva and let her know," I say. "I don't have a plan yet, and there isn't much time, so we'll have to think of something fast."

"I'll be over first thing in the morning. I'll get Jerome to drive Viva and me."

And for the first time in my life, I know that

Lonnie, Viva, and I have something to do that is more important than breaking a record, and just like trying to break a world record, I have no idea how to do it.

LARGEST VACUUM IN THE WORLD

I don't leave my room for the rest of the afternoon. I can hear voices downstairs—Jake's, my sisters', Aunt Ursula's. I wonder what she's telling them.

A little while later Dad comes home, then Mom. I still don't come downstairs. There's a knock on my door. "Teddy? Can I come in?"

Mom's voice is like lying down on the largest pillow in the world (61 feet long and 87 feet 4 inches wide). It's cozy, soft, and perfect. And just like that I'm sure there's got to be a mistake. Mom would never be a part of getting rid of the pigeons, so I fling the door open and before I can tell her anything, she says, "It's my fault, Teddy. I was the one who told my boss about the pigeons."

Strange but true, the longest vacuum system is about 33 miles long. I feel like the end was brought into my room and sucked out every single last particle of air. Even the air from the deepest parts of my lungs.

LAST HUG EVER

She keeps talking. "I was telling my boss about how Jake used to wear pigeon feathers, and of course I didn't know about the law, but when my boss heard about the pigeons, he demanded action. You know I can't break a law, Teddy."

"So it's Jake's fault."

"No, Teddy." Mom folds me up in her arms.

"What will happen to them?"

"They'll be sent away."

"So the only way Grump—I mean, Mr. Marney, can keep his pigeons is if the law changes?"

Mom nods. "But that can take months. The case would have to go in front of the city council. I'm sorry, Teddy. It's no use."

She might believe this, but I don't.

She hugs me tighter and this time I hug her back. I still don't have a plan for how to save the pigeons, and I'm still mad at her, but I do have a sinking feeling that after tomorrow, Mom

might never want to hug me again, so I better fill up on her hugs now.

LUCK OF THE POO

I have dinner in my room. I'm not ready to be in a big group, and Mom understands. For once, Aunt Ursula keeps her rules to herself. I go over the conversation I had with Mom. What I figure is that I have to keep the pigeons safe until I can change a law. It's the only way.

I call both Lonnie and Viva about a pigeon rescue.

Lonnie says, "It has to happen tonight."

I agree.

Next, I talk to Viva. "You have to steal the pigeons and hide them," she says.

I agree. It's clear that there's only one place to hide them, the only place no one goes: the basement.

And since neither Lonnie nor Viva can get to my house in the middle of the night, I need to do it alone.

Before Lonnie and I hang up, he says, "May the luck of the poo be with you."

I admit, I have not totally thought this through,

but it's clear that I'm really going to need poo luck to pull this off.

OUTLAW

Sneaking out of my house was easy, but I'd forgotten how dark it is outside in the middle of the night. I wait a few seconds for my eyes to adjust, and then move on.

In the back of the aviary there is a small wooden box that Grumpy Pigeon Man keeps in case he needs to bring a pigeon somewhere. It has a handle on the top and thin wooden slats on one side so the pigeons can see out. Six pigeons fit in the box.

I grab the carrier, scoop out some pigeon food into a can, and head into the loft, where the pigeons are all sleeping. I've never been here in the middle of night. When I walk in the pigeons fly up all around. I talk to them quietly so they know it's me. I've got a lot of work to do before morning and I can't make any mistakes. Slowly and carefully, I encourage six pigeons into the carrier.

I sneak out of the aviary. As much as I don't want to wake anyone in my family, I also don't want to wake Grumpy Pigeon Man. I know enough about rules to know that this will only work if he knows nothing about it. I slip up the back stairs, past Aunt Ursula and Peanut, and then to the top of the basement.

This is where my plan gets tricky, because even though I know it's crazy I'm still scared of zombies. From inside the box, a pigeon gives a coo. I take a deep breath, flick on the basement light, and slowly walk down.

OUTLAW PART 2

To keep myself calm I Darth Vader breathe, which this time doesn't work because all it does is scare me more. I make it to the bottom step and freeze.

A pigeon coos again and I remember who this is for. I plunge to the back of the basement. The safest place for the pigeons.

I let the pigeons out as far back in the basement as I dare go, leave some food, then run upstairs, closing the door behind me. I go out to the aviary and start again.

Each time I walk into the basement I get a little more nervous. I'm walking to the back when something brushes my face. I stifle a scream as three pigeons swing past me, fluttering in my face.

On the ninth trip out to the aviary, the sun is beginning to rise. I'm so close to being done. There are only three pigeons left. Princess Leia, Obi-Wan Kenobi, and a small brown-and-white pigeon we never named.

I'm sneaking past Aunt Ursula's room when one of the pigeons start frantically cooing. I freeze in my spot. Peanut barks. My heart leaps into my head, pounding like the world record for the largest Japanese drum ensemble (3,437 people).

Aunt Ursula says, "Who's there?"

I didn't plan for this. My brain is trying to figure out what to say but with all that pounding, it's hard to hear a thing.

And out of the blue, a voice says, "It's me, Jake."

And I'm pretty sure he just earned a new nickname: The Constructor.

MR. MARNEY'S BIRDS

"Jake, go back to bed," Aunt Ursula mumbles, but doesn't come out.

"I'm getting a glass of water," Jake says, and motions me away.

Jake catches up with me at the top of the basement stairs. I feel really torn about him being here. I mean, I'm glad he came to my rescue, but I don't want to involve him in my plan. Although it's pretty much too late for that, so I open the basement door and let him go first.

"Who are these ones?" Jake asks when we get to the back of the basement. The pigeons perch on boxes, on a trunk, on a table in the corner, and even on the water heater.

"Princess Leia." She flaps to her friends. "Obi-Wan Kenobi." He joins Leia. "And this one doesn't have a name yet." I look at the pigeon and then say, "Finn."

As I say his name, Finn starts flapping and lifts out of my hands.

"What about BB-8?" Jake asks.

I point to another little round pigeon that was also never given a name.

"Can that be Rey?" he asks about a pigeon off to the side.

"Sure."

Jake reaches out to pet her. "Are you going to tell me why you're stealing Mr. Marney's birds?"

"You don't know?"

He shakes his head. "No one tells me anything around here."

"Can you keep a secret?"

Jake nods. "I never told Aunt Ursula about loads of stuff that our sisters are up to."

"I thought you said no one told you anything."

He shrugs. "They don't, but I've got eyes."

And so for the first time in my life, I choose to include my little brother in my plan. And this time I believe he won't destroy it.

(Fingers crossed.)

OUTLAWS TOGETHER

I explain to him that I am not stealing them but saving them.

He thinks about this for a minute, then says, "You know, you're breaking two laws. The law that says the pigeons need to leave the city, and the law that says you're not supposed to steal."

I ignore him. "I just need to keep them safe until I change the law."

"So if I don't tell anyone, am I breaking the law, too?"

I'm pretty sure I've already broken Mom's rule about being a good big brother. So I figure the least I can do is be honest. "Yeah, you would be breaking the law, too."

BB-8 flies onto Jake's shoulder and pecks at

his hair. Jake giggles. Clearly it tickles. "Okay," he says. "I'll do it. We can be outlaws together." He puts his hand up for a high five. I raise mine and our two hands meet perfectly in the middle.

We tiptoe back upstairs. I look at the clock and see that it's already time for me to go to the aviary to feed the pigeons. Which will be weird since they aren't there. I hadn't thought about that part. I also haven't thought about how I'll feed them in the basement. Maybe Lonnie and Viva can sneak food in when they come over.

I'll figure that out later.

We go back up to our room together—two outlaws. I snuggle Jake back into bed. "Act as normal as possible," I say as I get dressed.

"I don't even know what that means anymore," Jake says.

"Me neither, but we'll do our best."

MISSING PIGEONS

I practice my surprised face on the walk over to the aviary, but I don't have to act because when I get there I really am surprised.

Grumpy Pigeon Man is standing in the loft with some man who could compete against Mr. Marney for grumpiest man in the world.

His fists are clenched, and he's speaking very slowly. "Where. Are. The. Pigeons?"

"They were here last night," Grumpy Pigeon Man says.

The man looks over when the door slams behind me. "Who. Are. You?"

Grumpy Pigeon Man says, "That's Tent Boy. He helps care for the pigeons."

I'm trying to act all natural, so I say, "Yup, that's me."

"Your name is Tent Boy?" Mad Face says.

"No, it's Teddy, sir. I live next door."

"Mrs. Mars is your mother?"

I nod.

"I'm Mrs. Mars's boss. And I'm here to take away these pigeons. But the pigeons are not here. Do you know where they are?"

I shake my head. "Like Mr. Marney said, they were here yesterday." And then, thinking real fast, I add, "I hope I didn't forget to close the door. That's happened before and the pigeons get out. It's hard to bring them back."

Mad Face turns to Grumpy Pigeon Man.

"Those pigeons better be found. And soon."

"But you wanted them gone," I stammer. "And they're gone."

"They are not gone," Mad Face snarls. "They've disappeared. We need to find them."

Grumpy Pigeon Man rests his hand on my shoulder. "It's all right, Tent Boy. You keep an eye out for the birds. We'll sort this out."

And then Grumpy Pigeon Man leads Mad Face out the door.

I'm left standing in the empty aviary. I've never felt so alone in my whole life.

CLEANING THE BASEMENT

The good news is that after they leave I grab a bag and fill it with food. I don't want Grumpy Pigeon Man or Mad Face to see, so I slip away as fast as I can.

And the luck of the pigeon poo continues because right when I walk into the house Aunt Ursula calls from her bedroom, "I'll be out in a minute for my tea and toast, Teddy."

She talks like nothing has changed and I go along with it. I dash past her room, popping bread into the toaster and putting the kettle on to boil.

Grabbing a bowl for water, I sprint into the basement to feed the pigeons.

I set up their food and then run back into the kitchen just as the toast pops and the kettle whistles. Aunt Ursula walks in. Peanut raises his nose in the air. He sniffs and then starts whining.

Oh no. I didn't think about him.

Right then, Lonnie and Viva burst through our front door, panting and out of breath.

Lonnie leans over, catching his breath and breathing between each word. "Jerome (wheh-wheh) wouldn't (wheh-wheh) drive (wheh-wheh)."

Viva is doing the same. "We (wheh-wheh) ran (wheh-wheh) all (wheh-wheh) the (wheh-wheh) way."

Aunt Ursula looks surprised. "This is earlier than usual."

I'm looking at the clock and thinking about how the pigeon food needs to be taken away in three minutes.

"We're cleaning the basement!" I blurt

out, and zoom away, dragging Lonnie and Viva with me.

TAKE A LOT MORE

Viva whistles. "So we've saved the pigeons."

Lonnie interrupts, "For now."

Viva nods. "And all we have to do is keep them safe until we change a law."

Lonnie interrupts again, "Which we have no idea how to do."

"It sounds harder than when we thought of the idea last night," I say.

Lonnie frowns. "I think saving these pigeons is going to take a lot more than changing a law. We just have to figure out what that is."

There's a knock on the basement door. Lonnie and I pick up brooms. Viva runs up and holds the door closed. "Who is it?" she asks.

"Jake."

I nod to Viva. "He's in on it."

Jake pokes his head in the door. "It's time to go."

"Where?" I ask.

"The mural!"

With all the pigeon stuff going on, I totally forgot about the mural.

We close the door tightly behind us. Smarty Pants weaves back and forth in front of it, meowing the whole time, while Peanut whines from Aunt Ursula's arms. "I don't know what has gotten into you today."

Grace walks over. She looks at me, then at Smarty Pants, then at the basement door, and then she scoops up Smarty Pants.

On her way past me, she whispers, "I don't know what you're up to, but you can count me in."

Then she stomps on my foot and leaves.

I can honestly say, I never thought I'd be so happy to be in so much pain.

GOOD LUCK

Because we're not in school Ms. Raffeli lets us decide our own groups to paint. And again, Lonnie, Viva, Jake, and I take a section close together. It doesn't make a difference because none of us says a word. Probably because the one thing we want to talk about is the one thing we can't talk about. I have to admit, I am really impressed by Jake. He's not making a peep.

The morning creeps along, but finally, it's time for lunch. Lonnie, Viva, Jake, and I sit in a clump far away from everyone else.

Weirdly, Jake is the calmest of any of us. He is peeling his peanut butter sandwich apart and licking the insides.

Viva sighs really deeply. "If we ever needed some good luck, we really need it now."

"Seriously," Lonnie says.

And right then, out of the sky above, pigeon poo plops with a splat right on the top of my head, and splashes on Lonnie, Viva, and Jake.

Jake smiles. "I'm not worried."

MAD FACE

We tell Ms. Raffeli we all need the bathroom. She only needs to look at the poo spatters to know why.

We head into City Hall to use the bathrooms. Viva's not here when the three of us are done. Lonnie looks around then turns down the hall with the animal control offices.

“What are we doing?” I ask.

“We need more inside information.” Lonnie makes the silent symbol, then slinks to the ground like he’s hiding from Storm Troopers.

Lonnie sneaks in. Jake and I follow. Because of the big counter, Mad Face can’t see us. He’s on the phone.

I’m not sure what we’re going to learn, but I’m doing whatever Lonnie tells me because he is the closest person to a Jedi that I know. And Jedis know how to fight Darth Vader, and right now Mad Face is my Darth Vader.

"I'll find those birds," Mad Face says. "If it's the last thing I do."

"The Dark Side is strong in that guy," Lonnie whispers.

Jake whispers, "Did you see the name on his door?"

I shake my head. I didn't even know Jake could read.

Jake points. And I see the name: Mr. Raffeli. Mom's boss is named Mr. Raffeli? How did I not know that?

"How many Raffelis can there be in this town?" I whisper.

"As of now, I only know two," Lonnie says.

"Do you think they're married?" Jake asks, as he tries to control a giggle.

Lonnie and I make gross faces, and Jake can't hold his laugh in. I put my hand over his mouth to stop him, but a sound escapes.

And all of a sudden Mad Face is staring down at us over the counter.

"Hey," he says. "I know you. You're Tent Boy."

Lonnie, Jake, and I back away and then dash down the hall, where we run straight into Viva.

We pick up our paints and brushes and start painting.

"You'll never guess what we found out," Lonnie says.

"The animal control officer," I say. "The one who hates pigeons?"

"Is named Mr. Raffeli," Jake interrupts. "Like Ms. Raffeli. And we think they're married."

Viva looks shocked. "They can't be married."

"Oh yes they can," Jake says. "Grown-ups do that sort of thing." And he shivers from the thought.

"But he's so mean," Viva says. "And Ms. Raffeli is so nice."

"Where were you?" Lonnie asks.

"I went in to see when the next city council meeting is."

"When is it?"

"The day after tomorrow," Viva says.

"But what do we even do?" I ask.

"A little less talking and a little more painting," Ms. Raffeli says. I jump out of my skin because I didn't know she was standing right behind us. I wonder what she has heard. Her eyebrows are in their normal place so probably nothing. "We only have a week to finish it." She walks on to another group as I slap blue paint all over the legs of a construction worker.

Viva moves her brush up and down along the same leg I'm working on. "The lady in the office says we need a grown-up and we put forward something called a proposal. The proposal allows for the city councilors to call for a motion, and the motion can amend the law."

"So we need a grown-up who knows about the law?" I ask, trying to keep it all straight.

Viva nods.

Lonnie paints a pile of books. "Where are we going to find someone like that?"

"I know one," I say. "But convincing her will be hard. She is definitely not a fan of pigeons."

When we get home, Aunt Ursula is reading the paper.

"Lonnie and Viva say they're here to help me clean the basement," I say.

Aunt Ursula smiles. "Such good friends."

Lonnie and Viva nod vigorously.

Jake promised to act as normal as ever, and he actually follows through and sits down at his weaving. By the way he keeps messing up I'm sure he's not paying attention to it at all, but at least he's trying.

Sharon is prepping some sort of food.

"Aunt Ursula," I say. "We need your help." Lonnie, Viva, and I sit down, so Aunt Ursula can tell how serious we are. Viva explains what she learned about the proposal to change the law.

When Viva's finished I take Aunt Ursula's hand. "Please, this is a matter of life and death."

"No one is dying, Teddy, so this is not a matter of life and death." She turns to Sharon, who is cutting up vegetables. "Not like that, Sharon. You want to curl your fingertips so the knife can't slice them. Like this." She takes the knife out of Sharon's hand and begins to chop celery as though it was butter. She hands the knife back to Sharon. "See?" Sharon nods, and Aunt Ursula turns back to us.

I pace the kitchen, because in an hour I'm going to have to feed the pigeons again, and I don't know how I'll pull that off. It is really stressful hiding pigeons in a basement.

Lonnie and Viva beg. "We'll do anything you want."

Aunt Ursula sighs. "The pigeons are merely being sent to other homes in different cities. They'll be fine."

"Fine? They've always lived with him."

Aunt Ursula shakes her head. "He knew the law."

"Okay," I say. "He messed up. But the ones who will suffer are his pigeons. They've lived together for so long. How can you separate them?"

Lonnie and Viva open their mouths but Aunt Ursula holds up her hands to stop them. "They're pigeons," she says. "They will survive. What I want to know is how he snuck all those birds away. Speaking of pigeons, though, I need to wash your clothes again, Teddy. I could have sworn I smelled pigeons earlier today."

"Ouch!" Sharon blurts out, and holds up a bleeding finger.

"Aunt Ursula, will you help me find a Band-Aid?" Sharon winks at me as she heads off with Aunt Ursula.

There is so much going on right now that figuring out why my sister winked at me is low on my list.

JAKE'S PLAN

Lonnie, Viva, and I walk away. "Do you think we convinced her?" Viva asks.

"I think she's convinced that the pigeons should live somewhere else, and that Grumpy Pigeon Man stole the pigeons," I say.

Lonnie raises a finger in the air. "Convincing her to help us is like convincing Han Solo to help Luke Skywalker. It takes work, but it's not impossible."

"So what do we do?" I ask.

Jake clears his throat. For a minute I had actually forgotten he was there. "We use the only thing she cares about."

"Peanut?" Viva asks.

"Peanut?" Lonnie asks.

"Peanut?" I ask.

"We need Peanut," Jake says, hopping off his

chair. He looks at Lonnie, Viva, and me. "And we need Grumpy Pigeon Man."

SMASHING ROOF TILES

Grumpy Pigeon Man doesn't want to come with us at all. We basically have to drag him back to my house. As we pass Maggie and her compost, she looks up and smiles at me. Again, I don't have time for my sisters. Especially because Grumpy Pigeon Man demands to know what is going on.

"To be honest," Viva says, "we're not sure."

I push him through the front door and plunk him down on the sofa in the living room, while Jake fetches Aunt Ursula. As soon as she sees Grumpy Pigeon Man, she turns in the opposite direction. But Jake won't let her; instead he pushes her into a seat.

Jake stands between them, pacing back and forth just like those lawyers on TV do. "We've brought you together because we need your help." Jake looks straight at Aunt Ursula.

"I've already told you," Aunt Ursula says. "There's nothing I can do. If Tom weren't such a stubborn mule then he would have taken care of this law years ago. And his pigeons would be safe."

Grumpy Pigeon Man looks at her for a good, long time. I tap my fingers on my knees. It's as tense in here as it must have been just before Lisa Dennis smashed her way through 923 roof tiles in one minute with only her hand.

I have to say, that would definitely be more painful, but being with Grumpy Pigeon Man and Aunt Ursula in the same room is painful in its own way.

MISTAKES

Finally Grumpy Pigeon Man speaks. "I've made a lot of mistakes over the years. Not fighting the law was one, but I made a worse one."

There's something about the tone of his voice that makes Lonnie sit down. All of us get really quiet.

"Ursula, many years ago—"

"Wait just a second," I say. "You guys have

known each other for many years?"

Grumpy Pigeon Man, Aunt Ursula, Jake, Lonnie, and Viva all stare at me. It's clear I need to keep quiet.

He continues, "You were so sure of yourself, and the world, and, well—how everything is supposed to work. And of course how rules make it all work smoothly. You know a lot about rules."

For a second I feel like saying something about all of Grumpy Pigeon Man's rules for his pigeons, but I stop myself.

"I wish I could make it up to you. Last night, when I learned that I was going to lose my pigeons, I realized what you must have felt like all those years ago when I didn't show up for our date."

"Whoa!" I say. Lonnie and Viva stare at me again. "What?" I say. "You dated?"

Aunt Ursula shakes her head. "No, Teddy. We did not date, because this man, as he just explained, did not show up."

"Ursula," Grumpy Pigeon Man says. "I promise I have no idea where the pigeons are, and I'm not asking for your help."

"Well, if you didn't take them, who did? They couldn't just vanish."

Before Grumpy Pigeon Man says anything Jake says, "Aunt Ursula. Help us or we'll call the animal control office."

Strange but true, the largest collection of Coca-Cola cans is 10,558. Right now I feel like I drank all that soda, and the sugar is rushing through my bloodstream.

"Wow!" I say. "I did not expect this." I look at Jake. "What are you talking about?"

"Yes," Aunt Ursula says. "What are you talking about?"

Jake pulls out a piece of folded paper. "This is from the animal control office. According to city law, you were supposed to register Peanut for a dog license when you moved here." He points to a spot. "Anyone who resides for longer than twenty-one days must register their dog. If a dog is found without a license then the dog may be removed." I hear a click of a camera and see Grace hiding in the doorway.

MORE OUTLAWS

And that's when Sharon, Caitlin and Casey, Maggie, and Grace pile into the room.

Aunt Ursula looks very unhappy. "And why are you here?"

Grace sits down beside Aunt Ursula. "You brought many new rules to our lives, and we're so thankful for them, but you never asked us about our rules. We have some Mars family rules we want to share with you."

Sharon clears her throat. "It's *not* right to *not* help."

Caitlin and Casey say together, "If you have the power to make change, use it."

"We all make mistakes." Maggie smiles.

Grace starts to speak, but Peanut, who is in Aunt Ursula's arms, starts whining, and then Smarty Pants, who is by the basement door, starts meowing. Grace glares. "Oh phooey, I forgot what I was going to say."

I look at the clock. Only fifteen minutes until I need to feed the pigeons. This is all taking much longer than I thought it would.

Jake smiles. "As Yoda and Lonnie like to say, 'You must unlearn what you have learned.'"

Lonnie gives Jake a high five.

Aunt Ursula clears her throat. "Let me first say that you have all made a compelling

argument." She stands up, passing Peanut to Grace as she does. Amazingly, Peanut doesn't even growl at Grace. "I didn't know about the law about dogs. I made a mistake, and I'm glad you've brought it to my attention. I do have power to create change, and because of that, it would be very wrong if I didn't help." She turns to Jake. "Perhaps you are right and I do need to unlearn a few rules."

I stand up and clap. I can't help myself. I'm so

happy. Aunt Ursula agrees with us. She's going to help.

"But," she says.

"But?" I repeat.

"That does not change my mind about the pigeons. Until those pigeons are found, I cannot help."

And now I'm just plain mad. "What have the pigeons ever done to you?"

"Nothing, Teddy, but they are outlaws. I can't help outlaws."

"The pigeons are outlaws?" I collapse on the sofa. "So what are we?"

LONGEST LINE

And right then, when I think things can't get any weirder, there's a knock on the front door. Sharon answers it and in walks Ms. Raffeli. She doesn't wait for us to say anything. "Tell me," she says. "What has my little brother done now? And how can I help fix it?"

Strange but true, there is a section in *The Guinness Book of World Records* about the longest lines of things. The longest line of toothpaste tubes (2,138), the longest line of ice skaters (370), and the longest line of tacos (2,013).

I find it very surprising how many longest-line records exist. But the news that Ms. Raffeli and Mr. Raffeli are siblings (not married), and that no one (like Mom) even bothered to tell me, is more surprising.

And then everyone starts talking about everything that is happening and what we will do to save the birds, and I look over at Grumpy Pigeon Man and Aunt Ursula, who both look so sad, and so alone.

I feel really bad for Grumpy Pigeon Man, but then I'm surprised again, because I suddenly realize that even though I'm mad at Aunt Ursula, I also feel really bad for her, too.

READY FOR DINNER

I'm standing in the living room, thinking about how sad Aunt Ursula is, and listening to Lonnie and Viva fill Ms. Raffeli in on what her brother has been doing, when Smarty Pants starts howling at the top her lungs.

"What's wrong with Smarty Pants?" Aunt Ursula asks. My heart starts racing because I'm pretty sure I know where we'll find Smarty Pants. I trot behind her. "It's nothing," I say. "Just Smarty Pants wanting dinner." But Aunt Ursula stays on her path, straight to the basement stairs, where Smarty Pants sits with her whiskers trembling and a paw squeezing under the door.

Aunt Ursula stops in her tracks. "Do you hear that?" she asks. "There's a distinct pecking sound coming from the other side of the door." She's right, there is.

"Probably mice," I say.

"And a smell." And before I can stop her, she opens the basement door and instantly gets a face full of pigeon. I guess they were ready for dinner.

FREAKING OUT

Right away, everyone from the living room plows toward us to see what's happened.

Smarty Pants runs after the pigeons, jumping up to try and snatch them from the air. Peanut leaps out of Grace's arms and starts chasing Smarty Pants in circles, knocking over Sharon, Caitlin and Casey, Maggie, and Grace.

The birds are freaking out. They don't know where to land, or where to fly. Lonnie and Viva

wave their arms in hopes of getting the pigeons back in the basement, but all it does is make them more frenzied.

“Stop,” Grumpy Pigeon Man says. “Please. Stand still.” Everyone does what he says, because he is Grumpy Pigeon Man, after all.

Grace grabs Peanut. Sharon grabs Smarty Pants. And as the room quiets down, so do the pigeons, who land on anything off the floor. Including all of us.

And that’s when Mom and Dad walk in.

PRINCESS LEIA TO THE RESCUE

Aunt Ursula doesn't even wait for Mom and Dad to catch up on what's going on. She turns straight to Grumpy Pigeon Man. "I knew it. You did know where they were!"

Grumpy Pigeon Man says, "If that's what you think of me then it's a good thing I didn't show up for that date!"

Suddenly, I feel terrible. I've messed everything up for Grumpy Pigeon Man. I just wanted to help. I can't stand it anymore. "I did it! I hid them." As I say this, the pigeons shift around the room, trying to find a safe place to land.

"Teddy!" she gasps. "How could you?"

"I love these pigeons, Aunt Ursula. I love their feathers, and the sound they make, and even their smell." Lonnie and Viva walk over and stand next to me. "And Grumpy Pigeon Man loves them, too. All I wanted was to save the pigeons. And I don't care if there is a law against them, because if I've learned one thing from you, it's that sometimes grown-ups make really bad rules and they need kids to set them straight!"

The pigeons flutter down on the dining room table, cooing to themselves. My siblings surround Lonnie, Viva, and me.

"You don't want to help. Fine. Go ahead and tell everyone where the pigeons are, make up rules for everyone else's lives, so everything stays neat and tidy, but there will always be a mess somewhere. You will eventually get pooed on, and it's not a bad thing because getting pooed on is good luck!"

And just then a pigeon flies up. It's Princess Leia, and as she flies over Aunt Ursula, she pauses for a split second and poos right on her head.

NOTHING WE CAN DO

After Aunt Ursula gets pooed on I run out so fast I don't even stop when Mom and Dad shout at me.

I run to the aviary. Without the pigeons it's just wires, and wood, and silence, and sadness. I wipe my nose, which, like my eyes, is dripping. That's when Mom and Dad walk in.

They flip over a bucket and sit down.

Dad hands me a tissue.

"I'm sorry," I say before they say anything. "I know I shouldn't have stolen the pigeons, but I needed time to plan how to save them."

"Oh, Teddy, I'm sorry," Mom says.

Dad lets out a deep breath. "We should have

told you as soon as we knew the pigeons were in trouble. Your mom was trying to sort it out, but couldn't. The council isn't interested."

"You mean we can't even put forward a proposal?"

"I tried, Teddy. They think no one cares about pigeons. There's nothing we can do."

I'm trying to breathe like Darth Vader but my air hole has gotten so small nothing can fit through it except tiny breaths.

Mom doesn't say anything for a little bit. "Teddy, what you did was wrong. I understand it, but it was wrong."

Dad moves closer to me. "We've got to give the pigeons up. You know that."

All I can is say, "It's not fair."

"I know," Mom says, and wraps her arms around me, which somehow affects the water in my eyes, and makes them leak a lot more.

"And now," Dad says, "about Aunt Ursula."

"I don't want to talk about Aunt Ursula." I wipe my eyes and sit up straight.

"She wants to talk to you. And you know the golden rule: treat others as you want them to treat you."

"I hate that rule," I say as Mom and Dad stand up.

Dad looks back. "No, you don't," he says. "You do this rule really well."

HOT PLATES

Aunt Ursula walks into the aviary like she's trying to break the record for longest distance walked over hot plates (82 feet 0.25 inches). It is not fun to watch.

The poo is washed out of her hair. She sits on the bucket Mom was sitting on. I turn away from her.

"I haven't been in an aviary for years. Not since Tom and I—" She stops talking, which is good because thinking about her and Grumpy Pigeon Man makes me feel worse than I already do. "They still smell the same, that's for sure."

I don't say anything.

"Teddy, you said some very true things about me. But what you don't know about me is that I do love you. And I do love your family." She waves her hand in front of her nose. "The smell is really awful."

I scowl at her.

"I'm not here to put down the pigeons. I'm here to say that after I washed my hair, Peanut and I went to the basement. We spent a little time with the pigeons." She reaches out and takes my hand. I let her hold it because she does seem really sorry. "I have to admit, the pigeons are very polite, quiet, respectful even, and except for the poo droppings, they don't seem disgustingly dirty. Peanut likes those pigeons very much. And he has excellent taste."

I pull back my hand. All of a sudden, I feel mad at her again. "So what is your point?"

"I can help you."

"There isn't any way to save the pigeons."

"Your mother explained the situation to me, too. But think about what she said. The council thinks people don't care about pigeons."

"And they're right. Look at you." I stand up.

"We have to show the council that people do like the pigeons."

"How do we do that?" I ask.

"Most of the time, Teddy, you have to follow rules, but sometimes you have to break them, and if you can break a world record at the same time then that's a very good day."

"I don't understand anything you're saying, except that you will help. So why are we sitting here?"

I reach out and take her hand, and we walk out of the aviary together.

BOSSING PEOPLE AROUND

Aunt Ursula and I rush back into the house.

We circle everyone together in the kitchen. There's Mom, Dad, Sharon, Caitlin and Casey, Maggie, Grace, who's holding Peanut, Smarty Pants, Jake, Grumpy Pigeon Man, Lonnie, Viva, Ms. Raffeli, and Jerome, who Sharon must have called right away.

Aunt Ursula looks at us all, then says, "First, we'll keep the pigeons in the basement. It goes against every rule in the book, but I can't think of another option."

Ms. Raffeli's eyebrows go up. "If there's any trouble, my brother will have to deal with me."

Aunt Ursula walks back and forth. I can feel her excitement. "The only way to change the councilors' minds is by doing something big."

"Like what?' I ask.

"Like a community event that proves to them that a lot of people care." She smiles. "We don't have much time. Sharon and Jerome, you'll want to do what you do best."

Sharon and Jerome look at each other and smile, then head upstairs to the bathroom.

Aunt Ursula says, "We need posters."

"I can do that," Grace says, as Peanut licks her face.

"Maggie, we'll need those posters put up all over the city. You must know a lot of runners."

Maggie stands up. "Aunt Ursula, I love running, but I think this is one of those times maybe the car would be better."

"Good point." Aunt Ursula points to Dad. "You drive, and Maggie will pass them out."

Aunt Ursula says to Mom, "We need to get a message to the city councilors. Tell them when and where they should be tomorrow. That is, if they want to get voted back into office next election."

Mom says, "No problem."

Aunt Ursula turns to Caitlin. "Cascy," she says.

Caitlin stops her. "I'm Caitlin. She's Casey."

"Really?" she says. They nod at her. "I've gotten it wrong every time, haven't I?" They nod. "And you never corrected me?" They nod again. She takes a deep breath and says, "Caitlin"—she looks at Caitlin—"and Casey"—she looks at Casey—"I need you to sew outfits for all of us."

"You got it," they say together.

"But after this—" Caitlin says.

"We're going back to our trash business," Casey says.

"We miss it," they say.

Aunt Ursula makes a face but doesn't correct them.

"What about me?" Jake asks. He's jumping around from foot to foot.

She leans down and looks him right in the eye. "I think someone in this house told me you used to dress up like a pigeon."

"I did. I did." He jumps up and down.

"I need you to dig out that outfit."

And he takes off upstairs to find it.

With all my family working on their assignments, Lonnie and Viva walk over to me.

Lonnie says, "It looks like you've got things covered here."

"Lonnie's got an idea that should help," Viva says. "We'll meet you tomorrow at the mural."

Aunt Ursula and I now stand all alone in the kitchen.

Aunt Ursula smiles. "I am very good at bossing people around."

And it's true. She is really good at that, and sometimes that's exactly what you need.

MAGGOTS

The next day I wake up early. This is the day. If we pull this off, we save the pigeons. If not . . . I can't even think about that right now. Instead, I feed and water them. It's amazing how having pigeons makes my basement feel a lot less creepy.

Slowly, the rest of my family wakes up and we begin to get ready. Sharon shows Dad how to cook the fluffiest waffles and eggs, humming as she does it. He doesn't burn a single waffle.

Next we all climb into the outfits that Caitlin

and Casey made for us.

"They're perfect!"

"Not as good as mine, but close," Jake says.

Caitlin and Casey explain how they made everything out of recycled fabric. "People give away the coolest stuff."

It's hard not to laugh, or think this is the craziest thing my family has ever done, especially when Jerome walks into the house all dressed up, too. "Lonnie said to remind you that he and Viva will meet you down at the mural."

"What are they up to?" I ask, but Jerome shrugs. "Beats me, I've been working all night on this costume. I can't believe I'm doing this."

Grace forces everyone together and takes about a million pictures. "Priceless!" she laughs.

Aunt Ursula is looking very nervous, and very serious, and also like she's about to throw up. "There are so many parts to our plan that need to work."

I know how she feels. "Breathe like Darth Vader. It helps."

Jake is extremely excitable and can't stop squirming. Maggie comes up to him with a bowl of dirt. She holds it out for him to see how she

turned the old food scraps into dirt.

"What are those?" He points to small Tic Tac–size insects wiggling in the dirt.

"Maggots," Maggie says.

"Maggots?" Aunt Ursula stops in her tracks. Everything gets very quiet. "Maggots." She blinks about a million times. "You have maggots in your compost. Throw them away."

Maggie shakes her head. "Maggots are the best. They're the pigeons of the dirt."

"No way," I say. "They're the zombies of the dirt. They'll eat your skin off." I don't actually know this as a fact but it seems like that's what they would do, like basement zombies.

Maggie shakes her head. "They don't eat anything that is alive. And they turn food scraps into dirt faster than anything else."

Jake's eyes light up and he says, "Cool!" And then sticks his hand in the bowl. "They tickle!"

I take Aunt Ursula's hand. "Is that how you feel about pigeons?"

She gulps. "At least, I used to."

I have to admit, if Aunt Ursula could change her mind about pigeons, then maybe I can change mine about maggots. But it's a lot to ask.

Aunt Ursula announces that it's time to leave, so we all climb into the van and drive to City Hall.

When we pull up, I see a pack of people: Lonnie and Viva, Ms. Raffeli, Lewis, Ny, Angus, the two Jasmines, Cornelio, the buddies, and all the other kids from the mural project.

I slowly climb out of the car and I can't believe what else I see.

The outside wall of City Hall, the one we've been painting with workers, is now also painted with pigeons. All around the people doing jobs are pigeons. It's like the people in the mural can't move because of all the pigeons.

Pigeons standing, pigeons flying, pigeons carrying messages, pigeons doing flips, pigeons eating, pigeons bathing, and, of course, pigeons pooing.

Ny waves. "We're going to add pigeon facts later!"

"Pigeons are so much easier to draw than people," Angus yells.

Lewis hollers, "I was going to say that."

Jasmine B. and Jasmine H. splatter paint on him. "No, you weren't!"

Viva waves. "It was Lonnie's idea. He's totally got the Force."

Lonnie yells, "Like Obi-Wan Kenobi said, 'The Force is what gives a Jedi his power. It binds the galaxy together.'"

I yell back to Lonnie. "But it's up to the Jedi to decide to use the Force for good or evil."

"Hurry, Teddy, you have to see this." Jake pulls me around the corner into the parking lot, and even though I knew what we were trying to do, I really can't believe my eyes.

Hundreds of people dressed up as pigeons! I see friends of my sisters', kids I go to school with, people I don't know, Lonnie's parents, and even Viva's, and everyone is dressed up like pigeons!

GROUP RECORDS

Strange but true, my least favorite records are the kinds where a whole bunch of people do something at the same time. I've always had a rule that group records don't really count as breaking a record. But now that I am here, in the middle of all these people, I realize I've been wrong.

And then one person starts cooing, and everyone copies, and pretty soon the only sound is coos. It's the noisiest and quietest moment of my life.

And that's when I know for sure that like Aunt Ursula letting go of her rules, it's time I did the same.

I join the group. Cooing my head off.

PIGEONS RULE

"Tent Boy!" Grumpy Pigeon Man strides around the corner.

He's dressed up like a pigeon, too!

"Tent Boy," he grumps. "You're the only person I know who could think of such an embarrassing way to save my pigeons. I don't know how you come up with ideas like this."

And before I can tell him it was actually Aunt Ursula's idea, she pulls me away and hands me a microphone.

"Where did you get this?" I ask.

"You know my rule about always being prepared. I had a feeling we might need it. I also have snacks and a water bottle." She plants a firm hand on my shoulder and pushes me onto a podium. "You better say something since everyone is here to help your pigeons."

"What?" I gulp. "I don't talk to crowds." I jump off the podium.

"Don't worry, Teddy," she says. "You love those pigeons. Just speak from your heart."

My mouth goes dry. My heart beats fast. My mind goes blank. These are all the things that happened back in school. And then I look out and see Lonnie and Viva. I feel them sending me the Force. I look at everyone dressed up like pigeons, and I remember why I'm here. It has nothing to do with me, and everything to do with the pigeons.

I hold up the microphone. "Pigeons are not

always liked, but that doesn't mean they should be outlawed." I look out and see Mom and Dad and my siblings. I see Jake and Grumpy Pigeon Man.

"We are here today to show our support for pigeons. We're here to tell our city councilors to change the law banning pigeons as pets, because pigeons should have a right to live in this city, just like any other animal!" And because I wasn't actually prepared to make a speech, I have to think for a couple of seconds of what to say next. I see Ms. Raffeli and Aunt Ursula and I know what to say.

"Here's why pigeons rule. Number one: They are related to doves. Two: Doves are the symbol of peace. Three: Pigeons know how to find their way back home. Four: Pigeons are gentle. Five: Pigeon poo is one of the best garden fertilizers you can get. Six: It's good luck to be pooed on by a pigeon but not any other bird."

At this point, I have to stop because everyone is laughing.

"I should know," I add. "I get pooed on a lot." And then I pause and look out at the sea of people, most of whom I don't even know but who are all dressed up like pigeons, and I have to clear my throat before I can say the last rule.

"And seven: Pigeons care for each other like family."

RULES ABOUT BROTHERS

Because that's about all I can think of, I finish up by saying, "Please, let's change this law before anyone in our city loses their pigeons."

A huge coo rises from the pigeons all around me. Aunt Ursula taps me on the arm. "Good job," she says as I step down.

Mom walks up next to me, followed by four grown-ups. "Teddy, these are four of the city councilors. They have something they'd like to say to the crowd." Mom looks very happy. She leans over and says, "I guess this got their attention."

The councilors step up. One of them says, "I am proud to be part of this outpouring of public support for the pigeons of this city, and for our city to be part of a world-record-breaking attempt."

Another one steps up. “Because of you, we have decided to reconsider this law at our next meeting. Until that time, we will place a stay on the law. This means that anyone owning pigeons will be allowed to keep them until we review the situation.”

Loud coos of pleasure erupt from the crowd. Aunt Ursula screams, “WE DID IT!!!!” She hugs me, and then goes on to hug Mom, and Dad, and a bunch of other people I’m pretty sure she doesn’t know.

Jake runs straight toward me and wraps his arms and legs around me so tightly I think maybe he could break a record.

There’s a lot I’ve learned in the past few days, and one is a rule about brothers. A lot of the time you might not want them around, but then, it turns out, you do.

WHAT I SEE

Grace is clicking away with her camera while Peanut hangs out in her backpack barking at all the people dressed as pigeons. “This is great,” she yells to me. “I think there has to be a record here.”

Maggie runs over. "I love this! I'm thinking maybe I'll run a marathon in this outfit. I could break a record for that!" She dashes away to find some friends.

Caitlin and Casey are biking around collecting trash from people, because with so many people, there's a lot of trash. It's funny to see pigeons collecting trash. They wave to me as they bike past.

And right then Sharon and Jerome climb onto the podium. Everyone quiets down as they start to sing together. "Morning has brooo-ken like the first mooooo-or-ning. Pigeons have spoooo-ken like the first bird."

I know it's super goofy, but I have to wipe my eyes. Maybe it's allergies, but I think it's actually Sharon and Jerome singing together that makes me feel record-breaking happy.

I see Lonnie and Viva waving from the mural, which is almost done, and friends from school painting away. I see Grumpy Pigeon Man holding Aunt Ursula in his arms.

Yuck! I didn't actually want to see that. I mean, sure, I'm happy for them, but really, yuck!

I look away and see Jake plunge his hands into a bucket of blue paint. Oh no! I think he's back to being The Destructor.

And then I see Mr. Raffeli charging toward Grumpy Pigeon Man and Aunt Ursula, and trailing behind him are Grace and Peanut, and it's clear that none of them is happy.

THE DESTRUCTOR STRIKES BACK

"Is that your dog?" Mr. Raffeli points to Peanut.

I run over. Lonnie and Viva are right behind me.

Aunt Ursula scoops up Peanut, cuddling him protectively. "It is. This is Peanut."

"Do you have a dog license?" Mr. Rafelli yells again.

"I just found out about the law yesterday afternoon. Your offices were already closed. I was going to come in—"

Mr. Raffeli interrupts. "No, this is too much! No one is taking the rules seriously. You need to give me that dog this instant."

Mr. Raffeli reaches out for Peanut, who growls. Aunt Ursula pleads, "Stop."

"You can't take Peanut!" Grace looks like she's about to stomp on both of Mr. Raffeli's feet.

Ms. Raffeli hurries over. "Oh, Walter, really, people make mistakes. Breathe, Walter, breathe."

"No mistake was made," he replies. "The rule about dogs is very clear."

Grumpy Pigeon Man steps forward. "Actually, there is a mistake." He pulls out his wallet and takes out a slip of paper. "I took out the dog license when you first moved in, Ursula."

"You did?" she says, and flutters her eyes.

Grumpy Pigeon Man clears his throat a couple of times. "Well, I know what it's like with that Mars family. You can't even think with all the ruckus they make."

Out of the crowd Jake appears, tearing along with his bright-blue hands straight out in front of him. He barrels into Mr. Raffeli, pushing him again and again away from Peanut. "You can't have him!" Jake hollers, and with each push he leaves behind two blue handprints.

I know I shouldn't be happy that The Destructor is back, but I am. I really, really am.

"I'll take it from here," Ms. Raffeli says as she drags Mr. Rafelli away. "I have an extra pigeon costume in the car. They're trying to break a record and need all the help they can get."

Grumpy Pigeon Man and Aunt Ursula look at each other like Mom and Dad sometimes do, and

Sharon and Jerome always do.

"Let's get out of here," I say to Grace, Lonnie, Viva, and The Destructor. "Before it gets any grosser." They nod vigorously, so I know we're all in agreement.

BREAKING A RECORD

The good thing about the blue paint that Jake dipped his hands into is that it dries fast, which is why when I help Jake into the tree he doesn't leave any handprints on me or the tree.

Lonnie, Viva, Jake, and I are all sitting in a tree. A while ago, Grumpy Pigeon Man told me how sometimes you have to climb a tree. At that time, I didn't know how right he was.

"This is the best view," Viva says.

"We can see everyone," Lonnie says.

Jake giggles. "People dressed as pigeons is really funny."

I dangle my legs over the side of the limb. My toes wiggle from happiness.

It's funny watching Maggie and Grace hustling around documenting this. Maggie groups people in bundles of ten, and Grace takes pictures.

“I’ve counted up to six hundred eighty people!” Maggie shouts at us.

“I’ve got the proof!” Grace hollers. Together they’re going to submit the application. I don’t think I’ve ever seen either of them this excited.

I know everyone thinks that all I care about is breaking a record, but it’s not true. I mean, what could be better than right now? I’m dressed up like a pigeon, sitting in a tree with my two best friends and my little brother, surrounded by pigeon people, and best of all, today we saved Grumpy Pigeon Man’s pigeons.

There's nothing better than that.

"How about longest time spent in a tree?" I ask.

"How about most trees climbed?" Viva adds.

"How about longest time to hang from a branch of a tree?" Lonnie suggests.

Of course, being here right now is amazing, but breaking a world record with Lonnie and Viva would actually be really good.

And luckily, we have the rest of the summer to try.

TENT BOY, GRUMPY PIGEON MAN, AND THE DESTRUCTOR

As soon as we get home, Grumpy Pigeon Man and I move all the pigeons back to their aviary.

I can tell how happy they are by their soft coos and happy little flutters. Peanut is happy, too, because he's with us in the aviary sitting very still because Finn is perched on his head. Smarty Pants meows at the fence.

Grumpy Pigeon Man pulls up a bucket and sits. I do the same. He reaches his hand out and Han Solo flies over.

"You did good, Tent Boy," he grumps at me. He's the only person I know who can say something nice but sound grouchy about it. And then a smile as wide as the widest river (the Amazon) stretches across Grumpy Pigeon Man's face. "I mean it."

We sit without talking for a minute.

"I hear Jake starts at your school in September."

I nod. "He's going to be great. Don't you think?"

Grumpy Pigeon Man nods. "I do. He's really growing up." Then he frowns. "Except for that paint business today. But I'm sure he won't do anything like that at school."

At this very moment, Jake streaks through Grumpy Pigeon Man's yard. "I don't want a bath!" he screams, and crashes into the aviary. He's wearing Dad's old white bathrobe and a white shower cap on his head, and he's carrying a bucket and a big spoon. Jake hides behind me. "Don't tell her I'm here."

"What's with the new outfit?" I ask.

"It's good, right?" He smiles. "I'm Maggot Man!"

"Jake!" Aunt Ursula calls from our backyard. "Jake! Get back here. There are rules about this sort of thing!"

He shakes his head at me. "I've got to feed the maggots," he whispers. He leans down and scrapes up pigeon poo from the floor of the aviary. "No one fed those little guys today. We were so busy with your pigeons." He looks at Grumpy Pigeon Man as if it's his fault. "Maggie told me," he explains as he dumps the pigeon poo into the bucket. "Maggots love pigeon poo."

"Guano," Grumpy Pigeon Man says. "It's called guano."

Aunt Ursula calls from our yard. "Teddy! Tom! Have you seen Jake?"

His eyes get big. "Please," he whispers. "The maggots need me."

I think about the short time ago when he sat quietly at the table weaving. It was so peaceful.

Then I push him into the part of the aviary that has walls, but still a lot of poo.

I look at Grumpy Pigeon Man, who shrugs.

"Jake's not here," I call back. "It's just me, Grumpy Pigeon Man, and The Destructor."

"Maggot Man!" The Destructor shouts at the top of his lungs, totally giving himself away. "Call me Maggot Man!"

RULES FOR LIVING TOGETHER

1. If someone needs the bathroom, let her use it.
2. If dinner needs cooking, help make it.
3. If someone needs a hug, give it.
4. If you get into a fight, say you're sorry.
5. If you live with a bunch of nut-oes, you have to let them be nut-oes. And strange but true, I'm fine with that.

RULES FOR ACKNOWLEDGMENTS

1. Thank everyone who was thanked in book one.
2. Thank everyone who was thanked in book two.
3. Apologize profusely if anyone wasn't thanked.

A LIST OF THE ALMOST BEST LISTS IN THE WORLD

Strange but true, making lists can be almost as much fun as breaking world records. Here are a few favorites from Teddy and his friends (Don't forget The Destructor!).

THE GROSSEST THINGS IN THE WORLD BY TEDDY, VIVA, AND LONNIE

1. Earwax
2. Leeches
3. Maggots
4. Snot
5. Spitting
6. Tooth grunge
7. Throw up
8. Throwing up
9. Ticks
10. Wet cat food

TEDDY'S RULES ABOUT RELATIVES

1. Eat whatever they cook. (It might not be so bad.)
2. Ignore their pets. (There's nothing else to do.)
3. They might seem like they're from a different world, but they aren't. (They've just forgotten they were a kid once.)

TEDDY'S RULES ABOUT LIFE

1. Stand up for what you believe.
2. Apologize when you do something wrong.
3. Listen.
4. When in trouble, talk to a friend.
5. When all else fails, breathe like Darth Vader.

THE DESTRUCTOR'S LIST OF REALLY COOL THINGS

1. Pigeons
2. Recycling
3. Maggots
4. Peanut
5. My brother

LONNIE AND VIVA'S LIST OF FAVORITE STAR WARS CHARACTERS (IN ALPHABETICAL ORDER)

1. BB-8—Funny robot
2. Boba Fett—Cool outfit
3. Chewbacca—Of course!
4. Darth Vader—His breathing
5. Finn—Brave, loves the Force, and leaves the Dark Side
6. Maz Kanata—Her glasses rock
7. Princess Leia—She's a princess and a fighter
8. R2-D2—Another funny robot
9. Rey—She's got the Force
10. Yoda—Duh!

TEDDY'S PIGEON TRIVIA CHALLENGE

Strange but true, Teddy Mars knows a lot of fun facts about pigeons. How about you?

1. What do you call a pigeon that flips, rolls, and somersaults over and over again?
   A. Dizzy
   B. Flipper
   C. Roller

2. What do you call a pigeon that flies the longest?
   A. Racer
   B. Tippler
   C. Forever

3. What do you call a pigeon that flips, rolls, and somersaults only once or twice?
   A. Tumbler
   B. Flipper
   C. Somersaulter

4. What is the name of the pigeon that is considered the fastest pigeon in the world?
   A. Bolt
   B. Lightning
   C. Felix

5. In what year did pigeon racing become an unofficial Olympic sport?
   A. 1967
   B. 1000
   C. 1900

Answers: 1. C, 2. B, 3. A, 4. A, 5. C

Collect them all!

"A highly entertaining debut. Delightfully rambunctious black-and-white sketches elevate the comedy, while Teddy's hard-nosed perseverance takes world record-making to hilarious new heights."

—*Publishers Weekly*